"I can give you anything you want."

Megan's hands clenched and her breath seemed to go faint every time she was in Gino's presence. Never had she felt such greed to be with a man.

She had no right to feel like this. Yet, it'd been so long, perhaps never, would it be so awful if she wallowed in it a little longer?

She'd stopped wanting so long ago, she'd thought she had no need left. No need to feel shivers down her spine. She needed only one thing: security.

But when Gino had taken her into his arms and spoke to her in the secret language of desire, it had been a woman who'd answered. Together in passion and need, there had been only a man, only a woman. One touch of his lips, and suddenly the impossible seemed very possible....

Dear Reader,

Every one of us knows that there's that special guy out there meant just for us. The kind of guy who's every woman's fantasy—but only one woman's dream come true. That's the kind of men you'll meet in THE ULTIMATE.... miniseries. This month, meet THE ULTIMATE LOVER, courtesy of Darlene Scalera.

In her twenties, Darlene Scalera lived everywhere from Denver to London and did everything from factory work to public relations for a top political official. What she realizes now is she was training to be a writer. Eventually, she returned to her birthplace in upstate New York. However, it wasn't until a week later when she met Jim, her husband-to-be that she finally knew she was home. Having learned that love is life's most precious gift, Darlene combines this principle with her belief "a miracle is only a moment away" to guide the lives of her characters. Besides her marriage, Darlene's Top Ten Miraculous Moments include the births of her children, J.J. and Ariana. She is now proud to add to that list the publication of her first novel. Darlene welcomes reader mail at P.O. Box 217, Niverville, New York 12130. For a bookmark and autographed bookplate, please include a self-addressed stamped envelope.

Regards,

Debra Matteucci
Senior Editor & Editorial Coordinator
Harlequin Books
300 East 42nd Street
New York, NY 10017

A Man for Megan

DARLENE SCALERA

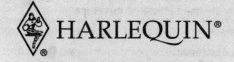

HARLEQUIN®

TORONTO • NEW YORK • LONDON
AMSTERDAM • PARIS • SYDNEY • HAMBURG
STOCKHOLM • ATHENS • TOKYO • MILAN • MADRID
PRAGUE • WARSAW • BUDAPEST • AUCKLAND

To my husband, Jim—
the man who made all my wishes come true.

ISBN 0-373-16762-8

A MAN FOR MEGAN

Printed in U.S.A.

Chapter One

The walls surrounding Gilgamesh were smooth. His own image was reflected in the shiny brown surface. In the past two thousand years, he hadn't aged a day.

Looking up, he saw a dome of thick glass. A face, blurred by the lid, appeared and was gone. He heard tuneless humming, then nothing.

No, don't leave yet, he pleaded silently. The sooner we begin, the sooner it'll be over.

And I'll be free.

He heard the humming again, and he closed his eyes in relief, thinking surely he'd never heard a sweeter sound.

He was not normally anxious for the moment he met his new master. In fact, usually he dreaded it, but this time was different. The source of the off-key serenade above was his two thousandth master.

His last master.

He had only to grant three more wishes, and the curse would be fulfilled. He would return to the Upper Tier triumphant and ascend to the throne that was now denied him. He would be King.

The glass top came off above him. "I hope I kept that recipe for that chicken and cream of mushroom soup concoction," Gilgamesh heard above him. It was a woman's voice. Gilgamesh recognized the accent as American.

He swore once more in a low tone. American females used to be so easy, but in the last thirty years or so, they'd refined fickleness to a fine art. Some were still easy, content with wealth and the promise of no wrinkles. But others wanted everything: money, respect in the men's realm and orgasms three out of five times.

In his groin, he felt the first ripple that told him it would not be much longer. The moment was near.

The hand that held the rim was red and chapped with several tiny cuts in various stages of healing across the knuckles. The nails were clipped short, and the veins popped out along the backside like blue bolts of lightning.

It was almost time.

MEGAN KELLY pushed back a stray curl while she eyed the crock pot. Cleaned up, it didn't look so bad. Her gaze swung to the neat row of cookbooks wedged between the microwave and the wall. She pulled out a thin volume, riffling its pages. She rubbed her eyes. She wasn't sure what she needed more: sleep or a meal started so that when she woke she had something hot to put in her stomach. She needed both if she was going to work the three-to-eleven shift tonight, especially after filling in on the graveyard shift last night. She couldn't say no to the extra work, not with overtime having been cut the last three months and her trying to save for the wedding.

She tried to read a recipe for meatless chili, but the words kept blurring together. Maybe she should just go to bed.

GILGAMESH WAITED, breath held, every part of him poised, ready to rise. This time, the wait was worse than any of the others. His lungs began to burn with held air. His muscles tried to twitch from their forced stillness. *Hurry,* he silently pleaded.

Then, as if in answer to his prayer, he heard the woman say, "Well, I should, at least, plug you in to make sure you work."

It was time.

The beginning of the end.

He looked down. His lower limbs had already dissolved. He felt his upper body engorge and rise, riding on the wings of smoke. Mixed with the heavy, misty swirls was the sound of the woman's panicked voice.

"Hank, it's Meg. Get the truck over here fast. The kitchen's filling up with smoke. I think it might be electrical. An appliance. I don't know."

By the time the smoke was re-forming into a solid mass, the woman was gone.

Gilgamesh stood on two legs as thick as tree trunks. He took a breath, sucking in the last wisps of smoke. He looked around the empty kitchen. "Okay, so I'm a show-off, but this is my farewell performance.'' He brushed a speck of soot off his Armani suit.

The screen door slammed, causing Gilgamesh to look up. His hands stopped their movement. The breath halfway down his throat caught. It had been two thousand years since he'd seen an angel. Now one stood before him, her hand lifting to her throat, her eyes, too large in a thin face, filling with wonder.

Her lips parted like soft petals budding, but Gilgamesh heard no words. The mouth slowly closed, the bottom lip caught beneath the front teeth. He saw a white edge where the tooth cut into the delicate skin. The sirens wailed outside.

He took a half step toward her, but stopped as she backed away.

''Don't be afraid,'' he whispered. It was not the voice that usually greeted his new master. It was too soothing, soft, without a trace of an immortal's ingrained condescension.

He eyed this new master before him. Yes, she had the burnished halo of curls and fine, straight features of the angels he'd known. She had the frame the angels were famous for—tiny and so delicately drawn you touched them gently or risked being left with nothing but puffs of glittery dust in your palms.

But if he ran his hands down this creature's spine, he would only meet the knotty press of vertebrae. There would be no wings tucked flat against her back, ready to unfold and lift her high above mortal men.

No, she was not an angel. She was only human.

He saw the woman's small, worn hand leave her

throat, flutter for a moment, then, drop like a broken-winged bird. He didn't realize his own hands had reached out for her until he saw them stretched before him.

"Megan May?" a man's voice called from outside. "What're you doing in there, girl?" The back screen door opened and banged shut.

The tiny woman jumped, her gaze automatically veering toward the sound. It was all the time Gilgamesh needed.

"Where's the disaster?" The chief of Shady Hook's volunteer fire department stood in the doorway. Other men wearing the same heavy yellow coats clustered behind him.

"I don't even smell smoke. It was you who called, wasn't it, Megs? Something about an appliance?"

Megan forced a nod. She was staring at the far corner of the kitchen where the man had stood. It was empty.

A voice came from behind the chief. "Last month, Gladys blew up an espresso machine. I'm still picking coffee grinds out of the carpet. She wants me to drink coffee in little cups, for Pete's sake. Where does she come up with these ideas?"

"You think that's bad?" another voice chimed in. "Do you know what Helen wants? A pasta maker. But can I get a universal remote? Oh, no, and there's a practical purchase."

Megan smiled wanly as she glanced at the men. She pointed toward the counter.

"I plugged in that thing there. There was all this

smoke and then..." Her gaze went once more to the empty corner of the kitchen.

The chief clomped over to the counter and examined the cord to the crock pot. He touched the metal prongs at the end of the cord. "I don't see any frayed wires." He patted the sides of the appliance. "It's not hot. Did this come from Henry's House of Hardware?"

Megan shook her head, her gaze still fixed on the spot where the strange man had stood. "Actually I picked it up this morning on my way home from work. Sal was selling it at his annual yard sale for two dollars."

Laughter came from the doorway. "I guess you got your money's worth, huh, Megs?"

The chief tested the sides of the crock pot once more. "It's cool as a cucumber now, but I'm sure you'll want to get rid of it."

"Of course," Megan agreed. "I don't want it sitting around the place. What do I do with it? Take it to the dump?"

"You can do that." The chief started to wind the cord around the pot. "I believe it's a ten-dollar charge for any electrical appliance."

"Ten dollars? I only bought it for two."

"You could have a yard sale," came the suggestion from the doorway.

The chief tucked the cord beneath the pot's cover. "Don't they have a garbage bin at the plant for non-recyclables?"

"They must." Megan stopped rubbing her forehead. "Maybe they'd let me stick it in there. It's not that big."

"I'm sure Elliot could take care of it for you."

"Of course." Megan's hand slapped her forehead. "I'll bring it to work with me this afternoon."

"You're going back in this afternoon?" the chief questioned as he started to walk toward the door.

Megan glanced at the corner of the kitchen. "It's my scheduled shift. Last night I was just filling in for Betty. Her daughter-in-law went into labor."

"No kidding. Did you hear if she had a boy or a girl?"

Megan was still staring into the far corner.

"Megs?" the chief said.

She looked at him. "I'm sorry. Did you say something?" Her words were slow, her tone distant.

"Is everything okay? You look a little pale."

"There…" Her hand lifted, the fingers pointing toward the corner. She had seen a man, hadn't she?

"Did you see a man standing there when you came in?" She looked away from the empty spot just in time to catch the expression that passed between the chief and the men at the back door.

"A man?"

Megan pushed the curls back from her forehead. "Before you got here, the smoke cleared, so I came back into the kitchen. When I did, I swear there was a man standing there." She gestured toward the vacant corner.

"I didn't see anyone. How 'bout you guys?" the chief asked the men. They shook their heads.

"Lou, come on in, and we'll have a look around inside just to be sure. You fellas take a walk around the house."

Megan stayed rooted, staring at the empty corner. She had seen a man. A man unlike any she'd ever seen before. He'd been as tall and strong as a redwood. His hair had been slicked back from his forehead, and it shone as if it had just been freshly washed. His skin was the color of polished teak. And he'd been dressed as if he were on the cover of a men's fashion magazine.

The heavy step of the firemen came back into the kitchen. "I don't see anything, Megan," the chief said.

"It was probably a shadow from the smoke," Lou suggested.

Megan faintly nodded. "Maybe." Except shadows don't speak.

"Unless there's something else we can do, I guess we'll be going now." The firemen started toward the screen door.

"Wait." The thought of being alone finally sent Megan into motion. She started toward the refrigerator. "Wouldn't you guys like a soda or something?"

"Thanks, honey, but no. We've got our monthly meeting and a quarter keg on ice waiting for us back at the firehouse. And you look ready to drop right where you stand. You get some rest now."

At the chief's words, her weariness rose. She hadn't slept in twenty-eight hours. She hadn't eaten in sixteen. In a few more minutes, she'd be asleep standing up, her dreams surrounding her like virtual reality.

Of course! That was it! The man she'd seen had been so handsome as to be unreal. And that's because that's what he was—nothing more than a vision of her overworked, sleep-deprived, caffeine-laced brain.

She smiled. "You're probably right. I better get some sleep. Let me walk you out." As she passed the counter, she picked up the crock pot. "I'll stick this piece of junk in the car right now, so I don't forget it."

Megan and the firemen started outside. "How are things at the factory?" the chief asked.

She shrugged. "They laid off ten more people last week. There hasn't been any overtime in three months."

"I heard they've got a few buyers from the South looking at it," one of the firemen said.

"I hear they're shutting down," another one added.

Megan shook her head. "There's a new rumor every day. Nobody really knows what's going to happen at this point."

"What's Elliot say?" a fireman asked.

"He says not to worry about it."

"Elliot's right," the chief agreed. "My father's worked there twenty-seven years and, believe me, this isn't the first time Crelco's threatened to shut down."

"That's what they said about the paper mill three years ago," Lou commented. "Then one Monday morning, the seven-to-three shift came in. They were met by security guards, escorted to their lockers and

told to clean them out, their severance checks would
be in the mail.''

"Taxes are too high in Connecticut," another fireman added. "All the plants are moving south. Who
can blame them?''

"All right, fellas," the chief said. "We'd better let
Megan get some rest so she can get to work before
the place goes under." He winked at Megan. "I hear
she's saving all her money so she can invite us all to
her wedding."

Megan smiled. "And you all better come."

The chief smiled. "Doris and I wouldn't miss it.
Elliot's a good man, Megan. I'm happy for the both
of you kids."

"Thanks, chief."

Megan waved as the truck pulled out. Elliot was a
good man, she thought as she walked back inside. She
went to the counter and wiped at the damp circles left
by the crock pot's rubber legs.

He was decent and hardworking and loyal—everything any girl would want in a husband.

So why was she conjuring up a sheikh in a designer
suit in the corner of her kitchen?

"Don't be afraid, Megan."

She stopped wiping the counter, and stood motionless. If she was the type to scream and become hys-
terical, she would've done so then.

Behind her, Gilgamesh's hands lifted as if to touch
the knobby curve of her backbone, but stopped.

"I'm not afraid of you." She started to wipe the

counter again. Her voice was of a child's trying to sound brave. "I know what you are."

"Really?" The last female master who had told him that had decided he was a male stripper sent by her friends and demanded he perform the Dance of the Seven Veils.

Not looking at him, Megan walked to the sink and folded the dishcloth into a neat square.

"You're a dream," she said, still refusing to turn around.

"Why, thank you." Gilgamesh couldn't resist. At least, she wasn't getting crazy on him. Screaming women were so hard to explain afterward to the neighbors and police. "My name is Gilgamesh."

The slip of a woman finally turned and looked at him. Her eyelids paused an extra beat between blinks. She steadied herself against the counter. "No need for introductions because after I get a few hours sleep, you'll be gone."

Gilgamesh forged on. "I'm a Jinni—Prince of the Ifrit Clan of the Jinn."

"So, you're the 'one-day-my-prince-will-come' guy. My mother warned me about you."

Gilgamesh leaned in closer. "What you Americans usually call me is a genie."

The woman's amusement released in a smile, her entire face becoming airbrushed loveliness. "This is a great dream," she said.

He smiled back. "Two thousand years ago, Ishtar, the Goddess of Love and War sentenced me to serve two thousand mortal masters."

"Really?" The woman's smile was fuller, more incredulous. "And why's that?"

"I refused to be her lover."

"Hell hath no fury, huh?" The woman chuckled, the freckles across her nose dancing.

"Ishtar loved only the challenge. Her conquests were more often than not discarded before the next new day. I had no desire to join her legendary list of humiliated lovers. Three times I denied her..."

He bowed low. "So three wishes you'll receive. I'm at your service, your faithful servant, the Genie of the..." He looked up to the counter where the container he'd come from had sat. "Exactly what was that thing anyway?"

"It was a crock pot."

"I'm the Genie of the...Crock Pot." He straightened and sighed. "I can't wait for this gig to be over."

"Give me four hours of deep sleep, and your wish'll be granted."

Gilgamesh smiled. He was used to disbelief in the beginning.

"As I said, you'll be granted three wishes. You can't wish for more wishes. Also, my powers don't extend to the realm of love."

"I know. I saw the movie."

"The movie?"

"*Aladdin.* I rented it one night when I was baby-sitting my girlfriend's kids."

"Please don't mention *Aladdin.* I'm never going to

live that one down when I get back to the Upper Tier.''

She looked at him curiously.

''My last master was an agent, and we went to a party in Hollywood. I'm afraid I had one too many Fuzzy Navels and got talking. The next thing I know it's in the script.''

''Your last master was an agent?''

''A literary agent.''

''A literary agent?'' Megan echoed, her skepticism asking him to go on.

Gilgamesh shrugged. ''Where do you think John Grisham came from?''

Megan burst into laughter. ''This has been a lot of fun, but I'm going to lie down now. It was great meeting you. Good luck with your goddesses.'' She started out of the kitchen.

''No, wait.'' The urgency in his voice stopped her. She turned around.

''You don't understand. You're my two thousandth master.''

Megan crossed her arms. ''What does that mean? I get a two-wishes-for-one special?''

''No, no. The curse was serving two thousand masters in two thousand years. After I grant your wishes, the curse will be over. I will return to my realm and ascend the steps to the throne promised me by Ishtar. I will be given the birthright thwarted by my mother's mortal blood. I will be King.''

Megan nodded. She bit her bottom lip, but Gilgamesh still saw the grin she was trying to stop. He smiled back persuasively.

"So, whaddya say? One, two, three, and I'll be free."

Megan filled the kitchen once more with the sweet song of her laughter. "I haven't had such a good time in so long, I actually hate to end this. Don't take this personally. You're a nice guy, and I'm sure you're going to make someone a great genie. But not me. Good night."

"Wait," he commanded, all persuasion gone, but Megan had already left. He considered going after her, then decided it was futile. He wouldn't be able to convince her he was anything more than a dream until she got some sleep. He heard her chuckling as she opened a door down the hall. "A genie," she said to herself. The door closed.

Scowling, Gilgamesh plopped down into the wicker rocker by the window. He crossed his arms. His fingertips tapped against his biceps. He'd waited two thousand years, he tried to reason. He could wait another few hours. He leaned forward, then back, setting the rocker into a furious swing.

MEGAN TURNED OFF the buzzing clock beside her bed without opening her eyes. She stretched and burrowed deeper into the sheets. It couldn't be morning yet. She rolled away from the sunlight trying to penetrate her closed eyelids.

Gradually consciousness came, clearing away the confusion of sleep. It was Saturday, she remembered, and she'd worked late last night. She was working tonight. She remembered the morning, the smoke, the firemen.

She remembered the genie.

She smiled, still refusing to open her eyes and surrender her dream. Beneath shuttered eyes, she summoned the man. He looked back at her with eyes so black she couldn't tell where the pupils ended and the irises began. His lips yielded with only a slight bow at the corners and crest. His cheekbones aligned in a long slant, lifting his features into a pose of regality.

She nuzzled into the down of the pillow. He'd been so real. She knew dreams didn't come true, but this one had come close....

She heard a loud squeaking.

Megan opened her eyes.

It couldn't be.

She got out of bed, wrapped a frayed terry-cloth robe around her and walked into the hall. The noise seemed to be coming from the kitchen. She tiptoed down the hall with measured steps, her heartbeat seeming as loud as the frantic squeak. She stopped just outside the kitchen doorway. Fear filled her limbs, preparing them to take flight. Apprehension heightened her senses until the squeak seemed to resound within her head. Careful not to show herself, she peeked around the corner. A dizzying wave of fright clutched her. She grabbed the doorjamb. Her throat swelled. Her lips parted in a gasp. The squeaking stopped. There, in the white wicker rocker, sat the man of her dreams.

The man turned and saw her clinging to the door molding. He jumped up. Megan let go and jumped back.

"Did you have a nice rest?" the man asked.

"You're supposed to be gone," she whispered.

"Make your three wishes, and I will be," he suggested.

Megan moved back until she felt her spine hit the wall. "You're real." Her voice stayed a terrified whisper.

"I'm in human form."

He must have been there the whole time she slept. Megan's mind began to spin out of control with fear and uncertainty. She could have been raped, tormented, killed. She had a lunatic in the house, and what had she done? She'd taken a nap.

She took a deep breath. Now was not the time to fall apart. She eyed the intruder. He didn't seem dangerous, but then again, neither had Ted Bundy.

"This isn't funny anymore." She marched to the telephone. "I'm calling the police."

"If you do, I'll disappear again like I did when the firemen came."

Megan stared to dial. "That's what I'm hoping for—your disappearance."

"Call in another false alarm, and the local boys aren't going to be so amused this time. They'll definitely begin to wonder what's wrong with ol' Megs."

"I'm beginning to wonder the same thing."

Gilgamesh sat down, crossed his legs and rocked

slowly. "Go ahead, call. When they come, they won't find a trace of me."

Over her shoulder, Megan looked back. He was gone. He'd just been there, but now, the chair rocked once, twice, then stopped, empty. Megan stopped dialing. She walked to the chair. She waved her hand between its scrolled arms, meeting no resistance. She patted the flowered cushion on its seat. Had a man been sitting there? The pillow was warm, but that could be explained by the midafternoon summer sun filling the room. The cushion was also squashed, but it had always needed a bit more batting.

She started to put the phone back. "I'm losing my mind," she muttered.

"No, you're not," came a resigned reply behind her.

This time she couldn't help it. She screamed as loud as she could.

"*Shh.*"

She turned around. The man was again in the rocker, his hands outstretched in a quieting gesture.

"Don't scare me like that." She released her terror in an angry outburst. She slumped against the side of the refrigerator. "How'd you do that? You're a magician, right?"

The man shook his head. "I'm a genie."

Watching the man, Megan picked up the phone receiver she'd dropped. She punched in Elliot's number. All she got was his answering machine.

"Elliot," she spoke into the receiver as she kept

her eye on the man rocking rhythmically before her. "Get over here quick. And bring your .38."

She kept the phone in her hand, her only available weapon. "Elliot was in the marines. A demolitions specialist."

The man stood up. She backed against the refrigerator.

"What do you want from me? What're you doing here?" she pleaded.

The man's hands extended in a pacifying position. "Like I said before, it's really quite simple. I got cursed, you got the crock pot. You make your wishes, I grant them. The curse is over. I get to be King, you get your dreams to come true. Everyone lives happily ever after."

Megan stared at him. "One of us has lost our minds."

The man's mouth spread into a disarming smile. "Freud once told me sanity is an overrated state anyway."

Megan's expression stayed somber, even though she felt the seductive pull of his smile. Inside her, something awoke, and her stomach went light. This response frightened her the most.

"Just because you're charming doesn't mean you aren't crazy," she told him.

The receiver in her hand was beeping. The mantel clock in the living room Elliot had given her last Christmas chimed twice, reminding her she was supposed to be at work in less than an hour. She didn't dare be late, not the way everyone was walking around on eggshells at the plant since the last layoff. Anyway, what would her excuse to her boss be: she had a genie in her kitchen? She might be losing her mind, but she wasn't going to lose her job.

The man unbuttoned his suit jacket and shoved his hands into his pants pockets, waiting for her to speak. She forced her gaze away from the shoulders filling his shirt, pulling it taut across a strong chest.

Elliot was the man of her dreams. This guy was just a lunatic.

She hung up the phone. "I've got to get to work," she explained.

"Wish for riches, and you'll never have to work again." The man winked at her.

No matter who he really was, Megan realized, the man obviously believed he was a genie. Maybe if she played along, she could get away and call the police from the pay phone at the plant. She'd get to work on time, and Shazam would have no idea the police were coming so he couldn't pull another disappearing act.

She tilted her head thoughtfully. "Three wishes, huh?" She opened the refrigerator and peered inside.

Gilgamesh came up behind her. "What is your desire? Strawberries picked before the morning dew has dried on their delicate flesh? Wine so sweet, it stuns the senses and casts all things real with a rosy hue? Pastry as light and crisp as meringue wrapped around beef roasted as tender as a mother's touch?"

Megan put a diet cherry cola and a foil-wrapped circle onto the counter. She closed the refrigerator door and moved away from the intriguing spice smell of her captor. She concentrated on unwrapping the foil package, revealing a pita bread filled with vegetables.

She took a large bite of the sandwich as she turned to the man. "I don't drink, and I follow a low-fat diet," she said in between chews. She popped open the can of soda. A light spray arced upward into the man's face.

"But I'm going to give your other offer some serious thought." Megan began to back away. She took another bite of the pita, spilling shreds of lettuce onto the floor.

She bent down, picked up the lettuce and put it into the garbage under the sink. "Three wishes. Gosh. So many choices." She plumped the pillow on the rocker as she passed. She'd almost reached the hallway. "I wouldn't want to make the wrong decision. How often does a chance like this come along?" She brandished her sandwich to underline her point. She was in the hallway finally.

"I'm going to get dressed for work now." She continued her backward retreat from the room. "But I'm going to be thinking of my three wishes every minute. Believe me."

By now she was halfway down the hall and out of the man's sight. She waited to see if he would come to the doorway. He didn't. She turned and ran the rest of the way to her bedroom.

In the kitchen, Gilgamesh reached for a napkin from the hand-painted holder on the counter. His lips screwed tightly together, fluting to one-third their normal size. His gaze stayed on the slice of hallway visible through the doorjamb. Slowly he wiped off the soda still wet on his chin. From between his pursed lips came a one-word oath:

"Humans."

Chapter Two

With a squeal, Megan's '84 Gremlin rounded the corner into the employees' parking lot, then screeched to a stop, backfiring twice. She generally didn't speed, but today she had made the fifteen-minute trip in six minutes. She glanced in the rearview mirror for the hundredth time. She wasn't looking for a squad car; she was looking for a magic carpet. What she saw was a square of blank summer sky. Except for the curious looks from her neighbor, Mrs. Schneider, who had been outside pruning her prize-winning roses when Megan had climbed out her bedroom window, the escape, so far, had been successful.

She was halfway across the parking lot before she remembered the crock pot in the trunk. Muttering all the way, she hurried back to get it. Balancing the bulky pot on her hip, she started back toward the plant, vowing solemnly to never go to another yard sale again. She switched the crock pot to her other hip as she pulled open the plant's putty-colored door. She took the steps two at a time to the break room, but Travis Smith was already on the pay phone. The way he was smiling into the mouthpiece, Megan knew he was on the line to his mistress. She waited a few minutes, but then, she saw him hook his thumb through his belt loop and spread his legs apart into a wider stance, and she knew wild horses wouldn't have helped her drag him away from the sweet nothings heating up the wire.

She hurried back down the stairs and into the side door of Quality Control. She set the crock pot on the floor of the employees' coat closet. She reached inside for a white lab coat, found a pair of earplugs and plastic safety glasses. She put the glasses on, but they slipped down as beads of sweat broke out along the bridge of her nose.

"Is everything okay?" Kitty Wasniewski asked in a voice matching the rushed pace of Megan's breathing. Kitty was the other Quality Control inspector. She was also Megan's best friend.

Megan turned around. From the corner of her eye, she saw Arnold Shelton, director of Quality Control, look up from his wide, metal desk.

"Everything's fine," Megan answered, upset to hear her voice too frantic.

"Tom and I heard the call for the fire department go out over the scanner."

Megan saw Arnold lean back in his chair. "You had a fire at your house?"

"No, no, nothing like that." Megan waved away their concern, forcing her own voice to sound calm. "I had a little trouble with a crackpot, I mean, a crock pot."

"That crock pot you just brought in?" Kitty pointed to the floor of the coat closet.

"What're you hoping for, Megan? To blow up the joint?" Arnold chuckled. "There goes this quarter's safety record."

"Don't worry. It only smokes if you plug it in. I brought it in to see if I could stick it in the garbage bin. Can you believe they want ten dollars to take this at the county dump?"

"Garbage." Arnold shook his head as he went back to the computer on his desk. "It's a gold mine."

Kitty, however, was still staring at the crock pot.

Megan picked it up. "Why don't I take this with me?" With her free hand, she grabbed a white bucket. "I'll go get the three o'clock shots." She was almost out the door when Arnold stopped her.

"Before you go, measure the Helman filter cores quick. The inside diameter ran below the min all last shift. I had to put their whole skid on hold. If it's not up by now, I'm going to shut the press down."

Megan glanced at the clock as she set down the bucket. The man would definitely know she'd escaped by now. She shouldn't have left him in the house alone. What if he got angry and busted up the place? What if it was all a ruse for a robbery? What if he knew where she worked and was on his way here now?

She measured the cores. "They're within spec, Arnold, but I'll measure the next hour's as soon as I get back to make sure."

Carrying the crock pot and the bucket, she ran up

the steps to the break room, this time breathing heavily with relief when she saw the room was empty. She set the crock pot on the counter, hooked the bucket on her arm and went to the pay phone. She was on the last number of 9-1-1 when she felt a touch, light, warm, moist, on the back of her neck. Fear crawled down her spine.

Two hands came from behind and covered her eyes. There was darkness, then a male voice whispered in her ear, "Guess who?"

Megan knew she had one shot only. She flexed her foot and prayed her aim wasn't off. Her heel came up swiftly, hitting its target. The hands covering her eyes flew off. She swung the bucket wildly behind her until it met solid mass. She heard a long, low moan, then the thud of weight hitting the floor.

She turned triumphant, but the victory in her eyes quickly turned to concern. The white bucket, poised to strike again, slid back down to the crook of her arm.

There, on the linoleum floor, clutching his groin and rolling back and forth across potato chip crumbs and straw wrappers was her future husband.

"Elliot!" She knelt down beside him. She tried to touch him. He pulled back.

"Are you crazy?" The words came between gasping breaths. "I give you a little kiss on the neck, and you try to kill me?"

"I thought you were…I didn't know who it was."

Elliot rolled onto his knees. "Who'd you think it was?" With a grimace, he straightened.

Avoiding his question, Megan asked, "What're you doing here?"

Elliot pulled himself up and hobbled to a chair. "I got your message and went over to your house—"

"You went over to the house?"

"Uh-huh." Elliot rubbed his right temple. "When I saw no one was around, I remembered you had to work."

"No one was there?"

Elliot continued to massage his head. "No. The only person around was Mrs. Schneider working in her garden. She wants to know why you're climbing out of your bedroom window these days." Elliot looked at her. "By the way, why are you climbing out of your bedroom window?"

Megan laughed lightly. "The bedroom door sometimes swells when it's hot. I couldn't get it open. I was running late for work." She shrugged and held her breath.

Elliot leaned back, wincing. He shifted his weight, trying to get comfortable. "Is that why you called the fire department?"

"Who told you about that?"

"Mrs. Schneider."

"Oh, right. No, I plugged in a crock pot I'd bought this morning at a yard sale, and it started to smoke, and I got scared, and—"

"You're still going to those yard sales? I told you, you don't have to buy other people's junk."

"It's not junk."

Elliot raised his eyebrows.

"Not usually," Megan amended. "And a crock pot is great, especially if you work. You throw the stuff in it in the morning and, when you get home at night, you have a nice hot meal waiting for you."

"If you want a crock pot, I'll buy you one."

"I was just trying to be economical."

"Haven't I told you before not to worry about money? I'll take care of all that."

"We've got to be realistic, Elliot. If the plant closes, we both lose our jobs."

"I said not to worry. I'll take care of the finances. I've got it all figured out."

Megan eyed her husband-to-be. She knew he made a decent living, and he was a hard worker, just like her, but this cavalier attitude toward money wasn't like Elliot. He was a conservative man in all matters.

"Money doesn't grow on trees."

"No, it grows in banks where I've been putting every penny. So, the next time you want a crock pot, let me buy you a new one so we don't have to call out the fire department. I'll never hear the end of this one on poker night."

"There was a lot of smoke," Megan defended herself.

"I didn't smell anything when I went in the house. By the way, you left the back door open. Again."

"You went in the house," Megan said, "and everything was okay?"

"Yeah, sure. The place is still standing."

"You didn't see anything...unusual?"

Elliot shrugged. "Everything looked like it always

does. I couldn't figure out what the big emergency was. Exactly why did you want me to bring my .38?''

The crazy man must have left. Her house was fine. She was fine. Elliot was…semifine.

''Megan?'' He was waiting for her answer. ''Besides the raging fire and the trapped door, did you have a wild man you wanted me to take down?''

She laughed nervously. If only he knew how close he was to the truth. But if the man was gone, and the entire episode was over, she saw no reason to worry Elliot. She leaned down and gave him a gentle kiss where the skin had started to swell on his forehead. ''I do seem to be overreacting to things lately. Must be prewedding jitters.''

Elliot rubbed his lower back. ''The wedding isn't until next year.''

''Can you believe I'm this excited already?'' She massaged his nape. ''Sorry about the surprise attack. How 'bout I make it up to you tomorrow afternoon with a thick sirloin, medium rare?''

Elliot's disgruntled expression began to disappear. ''With those little potatoes you roast?''

''*Mmm.* And fresh corn on the cob.'' Megan lightly stroked his hair. ''Strawberry shortcake for dessert?''

''With real whipped cream?''

''Would I feed you anything else?'' She was leaning over for a final kiss when she saw the crock pot on the counter.

''Elliot, I brought the crock pot here.''

He turned to the direction of her pointed finger.

''Do you think it'd be all right if I threw it in the

plant dumpster? They want ten dollars to dispose of it at the county dump.''

"The prices they charge nowadays for garbage. A smart man could make a killing.'' Elliot smiled as if the thought amused him. ''I'm on my way out now. I'll take it out back for you before I leave.''

''Thank you.'' She kissed him. He was smiling as she left the break room. She was smiling as she went down the stairs and back to work. It was going to be okay. The crazy man was gone. Elliot was going to take care of the crock pot. Everything was back to normal.

''HOW'S SHE RUNNING, WANDA?'' Megan said to the operator as she approached press twenty-one. ''The last parts I measured were in size.''

''Maybe the parts are running okay, but watch this.'' The white-haired woman motioned Megan to come up onto the platform.

Megan stepped up next to the woman and waited for the machine to finish its cycle.

Wanda glanced at Megan. ''You like Quality Control?''

''Yeah, I do.''

''I bet it's good to get off the presses. Although from what I hear, we might all be off the presses in another few weeks. Have you heard anything?''

Megan shook her head.

''I hope it's just rumors.'' The woman's face puckered with worry. ''I've been here thirty-seven years.

I've got three years until retirement. If this place goes under, who's going to want an old woman like me?''

Megan patted the woman's arm, the flesh her fingers touched as delicate as rice paper.

"Well," Wanda said, "we'll cross that bridge when we come to it. Wanna hear a good one? They called the squad out today to rescue a woman from a hot crock pot. That's almost as good as the time ol' man Myers blew up his work shed with a smoke bomb trying to get rid of a gopher.''

Megan was no longer smiling. Wanda, however, was still chuckling when the mold started to spread apart. Wanda opened the door, took out two long plastic cores and laid the parts on a lighted table behind her. "Now, watch," she told Megan.

As she reached in to remove two plastic runners from the left side of the mold, its large steel sides started to come together. Wanda pulled back her hand. The mold stopped in a halfway open position.

"See that." Wanda eyed Megan. "Last shift's operator cut her knuckles on the push-out pins trying to get her hand out.''

"The safety mechanism is failing," Megan said. "Put your blue light on. We're gonna have to shut her down.''

"What's the problem, girls?" the foreman bellowed above the noise as he came down the aisle.

Megan motioned him over. "Frank, we've got to shut this press down. The mold is closing before the door is shut.''

The foreman looked up at her. "That's impossible."

Megan planted her feet on the platform. "Nothing's impossible, Frank. What we've got here is a possible glitch in the safety switch."

The foreman shook his head. "A glitch." He puffed a breath of disgust. "What we've got here is an order due to be shipped Monday morning to our biggest customer, and we're already behind because your people put the last skid on hold. What do you want me to tell the plant manager when he comes in after the weekend and finds this order isn't even half-way finished? Sorry," he mimicked a female voice. "We had a glitch.

"Get down from there, both of you. This machine is going to run or it'll be my butt swinging from one of the mold hoists Monday morning."

"That I'd like to see," Wanda whispered to Megan as the two women stepped down from the platform.

Frank stepped up to the press as the mold began to open. "You two were probably gabbing, and one of you leaned on the door, so, of course, the mold would start to close."

He removed the parts and threw them on the table. "I don't know what you two are talking about." He reached back in to remove the runners. "I don't see any mold closing. Do you?" He looked over his shoulder at Megan, his expression bloated with sarcasm.

She saw the flat, heavy sides begin to slowly close like two fighters coming out into the ring. She pointed. The walls of the mold continued their slow-motion meeting.

Megan jumped up to the platform, her legs feeling clumsy and heavy. "Frank!" Even her scream seemed to have the slur of unreality. She pulled his arm, but she was too late. Three hundred tons of pressure closed on Frank's hand. Megan looked into his eyes. His screams eclipsed her own.

Still clutching his other hand, she frantically pushed the Mold Open button. Nothing happened. Wanda ran to call an ambulance. Others came running to the press. Frank was white. Sweat rolled down his face. He wouldn't let go of Megan's hand. "Help me," he whispered.

"Turn off the power," Megan screamed.

"We did. She's not responding," someone yelled.

The back door of the press opened, and two men started to unscrew the mold.

With her free hand, Megan found a frayed tissue in her jeans pocket and wiped Frank's forehead and fleshy cheeks. "They're taking apart the mold now. They'll have you out of there in a jiffy."

"My hand." Megan had to lean forward to hear the man's faint words. "I can't feel my hand."

"You're gonna be all right, Frank." She stretched her arm across his shoulders, supporting his body weight. "You're gonna be all right." She mopped his forehead, the back of his neck. "You're gonna be all right."

He looked at her and, with a shock of recognition, Megan saw agony and desperation dilating his pupils, turning his face into a grotesque caricature. She'd seen this mask before: on her mother's face right before she died in Megan's arms, in the nightmares that now woke Megan from a fevered sleep. She wanted to look away. She stared him straight in the eye, willing strength into her words. "You're gonna be all right."

His lips, thin with pain, parted, releasing shallow breaths. His eyes looked at her and said she was lying, then rolled back into his head, showing only the whites of surrender. His body slumped, its weight sending Megan a step backward.

"Help me," she cried. She braced her back and knees to hold up the heavy man. "Oh my God, I wish this hadn't happened," she said, half prayer, half plea, unable to look anymore at the face deformed with pain.

The weight of the body was suddenly gone. She looked to see if someone had taken the man from her arms and saw only Wanda, hands on her hips, who said, "See that."

Frank was gone. The mold was stopped, half closed.

"Last shift's—" Wanda began.

"Operator cut her knuckles on the push-out pins trying to get her hand out," Megan finished in a remote voice.

"That's right. Did Arnold tell you that?"

Megan shook her head, blinking slowly as she stared at Wanda, then the machine. She waited for Frank's yell.

As if on cue, he came down the aisle. "What's the problem, girls?"

Megan needed a deep breath. "We've got to shut her down. The mold is closing before the door is shut."

The breath she took stuck midway up her throat as she waited to see if he would agree with her or not, not sure which answer frightened her the most.

"Shut her down then. I'll have maintenance look at her. Wanda, help out on twenty-two until we get something else running. I'll go put the heats on thirty-five."

Megan stared at Frank's retreating back in disbelief. Her gaze lifted and, just above Frank's rounded shoulders, she saw the face of the man from her kitchen, the face that had been in her dreams. The man slowly raised three fingers and waggled them in a wave. Then, he folded a finger over, leaving only two extended, angled like a V for victory.

She walked toward him, not knowing whether she should be terrified or thrilled, only knowing she had to go to him.

"You're for real," she said, her voice echoing the amazement she felt filling out her face.

The man looked up from a casual inspection of his cuticles. "How do you think Oprah lost all that weight…twice?"

He was glad when he saw her bottom lip slip from beneath her teeth and curl against its top mate. It was an uncertain smile, but a smile nonetheless, better than the fright that had come into her features when the fat man was hurt.

He hadn't tried to stop her when she'd sneaked out of the house. He'd let her run away and had followed in another form, knowing she would run faster until she was ready to believe.

But, as he had watched her these last three minutes and seen the emotions shifting across her face like the changing shadows in clouds, he had longed to see that small smile once more. Now, it had come bravely, denying the confusion remaining in the rest of her expression. He smiled back.

"You're teasing me." The voice was unsure, but the tiny smile stayed.

"Yes, I am," he admitted. "But I am for real…in a manner of speaking."

"You saved that man's hand," she said, awe now hushing her voice.

"No, you saved that man's hand," he said, correcting her.

She stayed silent as if trying to understand what had happened. Her gaze moved past his shoulder. Her features were still, allowing him to study the slope of her forehead, the identical heart-shaped halves of her nostrils, the skin that rivaled the silk of royal robes. Her gaze came back to him with barely a movement of her head. Yet her curls bobbed as if happy just to frame this woman's face, to brush the soft rounds of her cheeks.

He'd seen goddesses and all of the great human

beauties, but, something about this face stirred him like no other.

Her features broke once more with a curious smile. "I've two wishes left?"

He awoke, returning to the reality that she was the master, and he, the servant. He thought how his father had been seduced by a mortal. Now he saw before him, stronger than his own infinite powers, the magic that was woman. Was she a sorceress? A siren sent by Ishtar in a final challenge? Was the goddess of games laughing at him now as she looked down from the immortal regions? He renounced the fright and fascination founded by the mere exploration of this woman's face. His attraction flared into anger, and he renewed his desire to be done with the curse and this wretched world.

"Yes," he said. "State your desires. I'll fulfill your every fantasy and be gone before the dawn breaks."

As he spoke, a woman with a bosom pushed up high came alongside the couple. She looked at him now with eyes unblinking. Her mouth was open, the bottom lip hanging low.

"Megan, Arnold's looking for you," she said. Her gaze stayed on the man. "I didn't know they were hiring anyone new," she said to him.

"I don't work here. I just came by to give Megan a hand." He smiled at his master.

"You two are friends?" The blonde turned a curious expression toward Megan.

"Actually I'm her—"

"Pen pal," Megan blurted.

The other woman continued to look questionably at her.

"Kitty, this is…is…" Megan stuttered. "My pen pal…Gen…Gino from…from Italy," she finished saying in a flourish of inspiration.

"Italy?" both Kitty and the newly christened Gino said at the same time.

"You speak English perfectly," Kitty noted. "You don't even have an accent." She looked at Megan for an answer. Gino looked at Megan, too, waiting for her reply.

Megan forced a light laugh. "I didn't mean Italy Italy."

Kitty's expression only became more confused. "What did you mean then?"

"Yes, what did you mean then?" Gino echoed, his enjoyment evident on his face.

"I meant…Little Italy…in New York City. Yes." She patted him on the back. "Gino is an American, born and raised in the good ol' U.S.A. Aren't you, Gino?"

He looked down at Megan. His presence definitely was a problem to her. Perhaps the bigger the problem, the quicker she would be to get rid of him. Besides, he despised the name Gino. "Whatever you say, Master," he answered sweetly.

Kitty's heavily colored eyelids flew up. "Did you just call her Master?"

Megan laughed nervously. "Megan. He said Megan." She shot him a warning look. "I'll see you after work, Gino. At home."

He debated, then decided he'd pushed her far enough for the moment. "I'll be waiting," he said, then winked.

Actually he'd be closer than she thought. Without the crock pot, he had to stay within five hundred feet of her at all times. But he'd explain that to her later.

"Goodbye, Kitty." He took the blonde's hand, kissing it softly on the knuckles.

"Goodbye…" He lifted Megan's hand, letting a smile play out before his lips touched her flesh. One kiss and the word was out before he could stop it. "Master."

"He did call you Master. I heard him," he heard the blonde insist as he walked away.

Megan joined the goddesses above in cursing him. "Megan. He said Megan. It probably sounded different because of his Italian accent."

"He doesn't have an Italian accent. He doesn't even have a New York accent, for goodness' sake. Where's he really from, Megs?"

Megan wished she knew the answer to that question. She watched the man's retreating figure. A glance around showed her she was not the only one who stared. The man moved through the plant as if he were a sultan crossing the common marketplace. Conversations stopped and heads shifted his way.

As if by magic.

Was he for real or not? He had turned back time and healed Frank's hand. She had seen it. She had experienced it. She could think of no other explanation than he was what he'd told her. But…

Megan had never believed in fairy tales. She'd scoffed at Santa Claus, rolled her eyes at the idea of the Easter Bunny. The only Angel she'd ever known was a biker chick with a leather bra.

No, while other girls were tucking their teeth under their pillows for the Tooth Fairy or wishing on a full moon, waiting for Prince Charming, Megan was watching for the new landlord, trying to think of a good reason the rent was overdue so her mother and her wouldn't have to move one more time. But the time would always come. There would be another run-down room, a new job for her mother, which never lasted, a new school for Megan with new faces staring at her and her ill-fitting clothes. After a while, Megan didn't even try to learn the other children's names because it didn't matter. She'd be gone sooner or later.

There were always men, too. A constantly changing parade of her mother's boyfriends, each one as far away from Prince Charming as possible.

No, not once, had Megan believed dreams come true.

Yet a man had come in a swirl of smoke. He'd stepped out of a crock pot into her kitchen. Without even breaking a sweat, he'd reversed the continuum of time and shattered everything she held as truth. With one smile he'd rocked her very existence.

A genie.

Her head told her to beware. Her heart begged her to believe. Just once.

"Master, huh?" Kitty brought her back to reality.

Megan looked at her, alarmed. "What?"

Her friend playfully nudged her in the ribs. "If I didn't know you were engaged to Elliot, I'd think you were getting into something weird here." Kitty laughed, walking away.

Megan watched the man round a corner, then disappear. "Honey," she muttered once Kitty was out of earshot. "You've got no idea."

Chapter Three

Megan was unable to concentrate on her work the rest of the night. By the end of the shift, she felt physically and mentally exhausted. She started her car, but sat there a moment, staring blankly into the blackness beyond the windshield. A fly was buzzing near her ear. She swatted at it in annoyance. She put the car into Drive, pulled out of the employees' parking lot and slowly started for home, not sure what awaited her there.

"Tough day at the office, dear?" a disembodied voice came from beside her. The car had been empty. Now, Gino sat beside her, seeming too large for the compact's close interior.

"Careful." He reached out and twisted the wheel to the left, pulling the car away just in time to avoid the guardrails.

Megan stared at him in disbelief.

"Shouldn't you keep your eyes on the road?" the man suggested.

"W-w-w..." she stammered.

"W-W-Wyoming! Beautiful country. Granted a

wish there for a man who loved his horse and hated his wife. Asked me to switch the two. Ended up with a wife with a horse face, and a mare that bucked him onto his butt whenever she had the chance. Ever see a woman with a horse face? Whoa, git along little doggies! But I think the mare found true happiness with a neighboring palomino. Just shows you, you've gotta be careful what you wish for.''

''W-w-where did you come from?''

''Look out. Incoming.'' The man turned the wheel again and swerved away from the pickup truck they were heading straight for. ''Maybe you'd better let me drive. You seem a little preoccupied.''

He took her hands off the wheel and folded them in her lap. She stared at him, not noticing his own hands didn't return to the wheel.

''Where did you come from?'' she demanded.

''I've been right here.''

Megan shook her head. ''You weren't sitting there when I got into the car.''

''I was right beside you.''

''The only thing in here was a fly.'' Understanding crept across Megan's features, understanding compounded by disbelief. ''You don't mean…''

''A genie can take on many forms, human or animal. You really should be kinder to even the lowly insect. You never know who you're swatting.''

Megan dropped her head into her hands. It swayed side to side, a shaking, silent ''no.'' The back of her neck arched, its white skin visible beneath a few fine scrolls of hair. Gino looked at the lady's nape and fascination seized him. He, in all his travels and times immortal, could never recall anything so singularly wondrous.

Megan released her head and looked up. It was then she noticed there were no hands on the steering wheel. She grabbed the wheel and slammed on the brakes, thrusting herself and Gino toward the dashboard. The back of the car fishtailed, then started to spin. Megan was screaming. It took several seconds and a sugar maple for the spinning to stop. Megan lurched forward, hitting the steering wheel. The screaming stopped.

"Look what you've done." The tremor in the man's voice matched the throbbing at Megan's right temple. "We were doing fine until you took over the wheel again."

She felt something warm slipping down the side of her face. She reached up, and when she brought her hand back down, it was bloodstained.

"Let me see." Gino's large hand covered her own, so she couldn't see the blood. His other hand lifted the hair at her temple and touched the wound, his fingertips as gentle as a summer breeze against her skin.

"Why I've done worse shaving," he said. He leaned back, letting go of Megan's hand.

The blood smeared across her fingertips was gone. She looked into the rearview mirror. Nothing, not even a scratch where the gash across her forehead had been mere seconds ago. She looked at Gino.

"It's on the house." He smiled.

Gingerly touching her temple, Megan looked in the mirror again. Farther back, in the darkness, she saw the flash of red lights. Two policemen were coming toward the car. Gino followed her gaze.

"You certainly keep the local emergency services busy," he remarked.

"Disappear," she told him. She was watching the police in the mirror. They were almost to the car.

"What?"

She looked directly at him. "Disappear." There was a tap on her window. She turned to see the policemen right outside her door. She rolled down her window.

"Good evening, officers."

"Ma'am." The taller one on the right shone his flashlight on her. "Are you all right?"

"Yes." The flashlight beam moved past her to the other side of the car. She glanced over her shoulder. The seat beside her was empty. "I'm fine."

"Megan?" The policeman standing farther back came up closer. "Is that you?"

She shielded her eyes from the flashlight glare. "Charlie? Thank goodness! How ya been?"

"Fine, honey, but an ambulance is on the way for you."

As he spoke, Megan heard the siren. "I'm fine, really. Not even a scratch."

"I'll need to see your license and registration, please," the taller officer on the right interjected.

"Megan, this is Kevin Connors, a new recruit," Charlie introduced.

"How do you do, Kevin? Welcome to Shady Hook."

"Thank you, ma'am. License and registration, please."

"Of course." Megan reached for her wallet. She saw a fly slowly making its way across the windshield. She handed her license and registration to the policeman. "I'm not sure what happened. I've just left work. One minute, I'm driving home, the next minute, well…"

"How's things going at Crelco?" Charlie asked. "I heard talk of a shutdown."

"We all have," Megan said. "Hopefully, that's all it is—talk."

Kevin shone the light on the cards she'd given him. He brushed at something on the license. Megan saw a fly lift off from her license picture. She glanced at the windshield. The fly that had been there was gone.

The young cop looked up from her license to her face. "You've been driving erratically for the past mile, ma'am." The flashlight beam veered as the policeman brought his hand up to shoo away something near his neck. Megan saw the fly in the shaft of light.

"I have? I'm sorry. I worked some extra hours this weekend. I've had very little sleep over the past two days."

She saw the fly land on the man's neck. She watched it follow the edge of his collar. "I may have—"

The cop's hand came up and slapped the side of his neck.

"No!" Megan cried.

The young cop stared at her as he took his hand away from his neck.

"You didn't kill it, did you?" Her voice trembled on the edge of hysteria.

Charlie took a step closer. He was looking at her oddly now, too. The other officer looked down into the palm of his hand.

"No, ma'am, I think I missed it."

"I hope so. You should be more careful," Megan scolded.

"Megan," Charlie said. "It was a fly."

"It was a living, breathing creature, wasn't it?" she challenged.

"Ma'am?" The full force of the flashlight beam hit her in the face. "Have you been drinking tonight?"

Megan let out a choked laugh. "I don't drink. Tell him, Charlie."

Charlie didn't say anything.

"Ma'am?" The other cop opened the car door. "Could you get out of the car, please?"

"What for?"

Kevin waited, holding the car door open.

"Charlie?" Megan appealed.

"Please do what he says, Megan."

Muttering to herself, she got out of the car. The young cop handed her an odd contraption. "Blow into this, please."

She eyed the small machine. "What's that?"

"Breathalyzer, ma'am."

"I told you I don't drink." Past the policemen's shoulders, she saw the ambulance pull up and the attendants get out.

"Then, there shouldn't be a problem." Kevin held the machine out to her.

With an annoyed sigh, she took the Breathalyzer and breathed into its mouthpiece. She handed it back to Kevin.

"Negative alcohol content," he said.

"Will that be all?" she asked.

"Yes, it will," Charlie said, looking at the young cop.

Megan saw the ambulance attendants coming forward with the stretcher. "That won't be necessary," she assured them. "I'm fine, really."

"You should be looked at, ma'am. You took quite a jolt," Kevin advised. Before she could stop him, an ambulance attendant strapped a blood pressure cuff to her arm. The other felt her limbs.

"Her blood pressure's a little high."

"It should be. I just slammed into a tree and have been treated like the town lush."

"Are you refusing medical treatment?" the young cop asked without looking up from the clipboard he was writing on.

"Megan." Charlie put an arm around her shoulders, walking her away from the other cop. "You really should be X-rayed just to make sure there's no injury."

"I'm telling you I'm fine."

"You may feel fine, but you've just had a serious accident. You're probably in shock."

It wouldn't be the first time today, Megan thought.

"Hey, Charlie," Kevin's voice called from behind them. "Look at this."

Megan turned around and saw the young cop leaning into her car, the flashlight shining on the steering wheel.

"What is it?" Charlie asked.

The other cop straightened, bringing his hand close to his face to examine something on his fingers. He looked up, his gaze zeroing in on Megan. "There's blood on the steering wheel."

For the second time that day, Megan joined the goddesses in cursing Gino.

Charlie looked at her, the spare lines of his face angling with puzzlement. "Are you sure?" he asked the other cop. He started toward him. Megan followed slowly behind.

One of the ambulance workers bent close to Kevin's fingers. "Yup, that's blood, all right." His eyes inventoried Megan. "Fresh blood. Not even begun to dry."

The other attendant wheeled the stretcher forward. "Miss, perhaps you should lie down?"

The four men stood in a semicircle around her. Four sets of eyes watched her. She knew they would never let her go now until she'd been thoroughly checked by a physician.

She sank down on the stretcher, surprised at how good it felt to sit down.

An attendant gently pushed her back on the stretcher until she was laid out flat. They started wheeling her toward the ambulance.

She sat back up. "What about my car?"

"I'll drive it to your house," Charlie said as he walked to the front of the car. "I think it's still drivable." He scratched his head as he looked over the car. "In fact, I don't see any damage."

He squatted down, aiming the flashlight beam across the front end. "Not a scratch. That's impossible. What kind of car is this? I've got to get me one."

Megan laid back down. In the black sky above, she saw a lone bird circling. It called out, a strong, beautiful yet hauntingly lonely cry. Gino hadn't abandoned her.

They opened the ambulance door and lifted her inside.

"When I get back to the station, I'll call Elliot for you," Charlie yelled, now examining the other side of the car.

She started to sit up. "That won't be—" The ambulance door closed. She sank back down on the stretcher. "Necessary," she finished lamely.

IT WAS AFTER TWO before Megan made it home. She unlocked the back door, but didn't go in. First, she reached around the jamb to the switch on the wall and turned on the overhead kitchen light. The room flooded with light, allowing her to check the chairs, the countertop, the corners. It was empty.

"Aren't we going in?" Elliot asked behind her.

She stepped inside. Elliot followed her. Perhaps she'd been wrong about the bird. Maybe the policeman had been mistaken about the fly, and he'd killed the genie. Was Gino gone? For good?

Beside her, Elliot yawned.

"I'm so sorry you had to come out at this crazy hour," she apologized again. "I told them I was fine, but they wanted to make sure."

"They were just doing their job, Megan."

"Yes, of course."

"Besides, you must've been bleeding at some point. Charlie said there was blood on the steering wheel."

There was no point in arguing, Megan decided. There had been blood, so, consequently, she must have been bleeding. It was simple logic.

Only simple logic didn't seem to apply to her life anymore.

"Still I can't figure out where the blood came from."

Megan said nothing. If she tried to explain, they would be sending the ambulance back for her, only this time, she'd be heading for the psycho ward.

"The main thing is—" Elliot wrapped his arms around her "—you're all right."

She didn't return his embrace.

"You are all right, aren't you?"

He wasn't holding her tightly, but still she felt as if the very breath was being choked from her body.

"I'm fine. Really." She wriggled out of his grasp and sat down at the kitchen table.

"It's just that you don't seem like yourself. There was the call to the fire department—"

"This kitchen was full of smoke at the time I called."

"And the crazy message on my machine."

Elliot was waiting for an answer. She was too tired to think straight, let alone wriggle her way out of this.

"Then, the accident. None of it makes sense."

For a minute, she considered telling Elliot the truth. He was, after all, her fiancé, the man she was going to share the rest of her life with. Certainly he deserved to know the truth.

She looked at him. Even at this late hour, every hair was in place, his chinos wrinkle-free, his socks the same color as his Polo shirt. He could have just come from a round of golf, below par, of course, instead of being abruptly woken from a deep sleep. It was one of the things that had first attracted her to him—his reliability, his dependability. She also knew it was this same practicality that would never be able to accept the idea of a two-thousand-year-old genie that may have just met his doom beneath a policeman's palm.

"You're right. It's been a long day. What we both need is a good night's sleep."

"It's so late…" Elliot looked at her. "I could stay here."

Normally she'd agree, but she needed to think

about everything that'd happened today and try to figure it out. She needed some time. Alone.

"I'm really exhausted, Elliot."

"Of course." He planted a kiss on her forehead. "You get some rest. I'll call you in the morning." He half smiled. "But not too early."

She needn't have worried Elliot would get mad. Elliot rarely got mad. Anger was a waste of energy, he said.

"Thank you, again," Megan said as she walked him to the back door. "I'm sorry you had to be dragged out in the middle of the night."

"Don't think twice about it." Elliot glanced at his wristwatch. He wore it at all times, even in bed. "I still have time to get in my recommended eight hours."

There was one more kiss, then he left.

Megan closed the door and leaned against it for a moment, her forehead pressed to the cool glass of the window. She could fall asleep right here, standing up.

"Buon giorno, señorita."

She was instantly awake. She spun around. Gino was posed against the counter, looking like an ad for designer cologne.

"You're still here?" Her heart was beating faster.

He spread out his arms. "In the flesh. Human at the moment."

"But I saw the fly, and then, the policeman swatted at it—"

"I've battled giants and beasts. It's going to take much more than a whack from a rookie cop to get rid of me. Besides, I'd already left that form and gone into another.''

"The bird," Megan said.

"Now you're getting the hang of it."

Behind her, Megan heard the creak of the screen door. The knob of the door she leaned against started to turn.

"Oh, no!" She flattened herself against the window, trying to block whoever was at the door from seeing in. She pushed against the door as it tried to open.

"Megan?" Elliot called from the other side.

"Yes?" she answered in a high-pitched warble. She gestured frantically to Gino, pointing toward the hallway. "Go," she mouthed.

He rolled his eyes heavenward, then vanished.

Megan moved away from the door. It swung inward, Elliot half falling through it. He grabbed at the door frame.

"Elliot?"

He righted himself and took a deep breath, brushing off the front of his Polo. "I thought I heard you talking to someone?"

"Me?" Megan squeaked. "Who would I be talking to? There's no one here."

Elliot tilted his head. "I swore I heard voices."

"Voices? Oh, I know. I was singing." She broke into a strained trill. "I dream of Jeanie…"

"It was a deeper voice."

Megan lowered her voice to a tenor. "I dream of Jeanie…"

Elliot stared at her, his brows pulling together, forming tiny furrows at the bridge of his nose. "Anyway, I just came back to tell you, Mom asked us to Sunday dinner tomorrow afternoon."

"Oh" was all Megan said.

"I know you and she don't always see eye to eye—"

"Don't beat around the bush. Your mother doesn't. She has made it clear on several occasions how she feels about me. The woman can't stand me."

"Aren't you exaggerating just a bit?"

"The last time I saw her, she said, 'You aren't going to marry my son, you're going to bury him.' From that statement, I think it's pretty safe to say your mother does not care for me."

"Now, now." Elliot punctuated his words with a flap of his hands. "I know that sounds like she doesn't like you, but that's just Mom's sense of humor."

Megan crossed her arms. "If she's planning on going into stand-up comedy, advise her not to quit her day job."

"You have to get to know her. That's why I told her we'd be there tomorrow. So you and she can, well, interact."

"You're killing yourself here, Elliot."

"I told her we'd be there at two."

"You accepted? Without checking with me first? You knew I was planning on cooking dinner for us."

"Now you won't have to. You can put your feet up and be a lady of leisure all day. You've been working too hard. Tonight you were lucky you didn't kill yourself. Besides, I want the two girls in my life to get along. Mom's making an effort. You can, at least, meet her halfway.''

Megan sighed. ''You're right. Your mother and I are going to have to learn to get along sooner or later.''

''Thanks, Megs. I owe you one.'' Elliot rewarded her with a kiss. ''And don't worry, someday soon, I'll give you everything you've ever wanted.''

''For now, just give me some suggestions on how to convince your mother I'm worthy of her only baby.''

''Just be yourself.''

''I already tried that. It didn't work.''

''Give it time. She'll come around. It's just that since Dad died, I'm all my mom's got.''

Megan closed the door behind him, locking it this time. She did understand, more than Elliot thought. Because Elliot was all she'd had, too. Until today.

''I dream of Jeanie?'' Gino asked behind her. ''Very cute.''

Megan sat down at the kitchen table. The clock on the wall said 3:10. She rubbed the center of her forehead. Weariness pooled in her eyes. ''Do you always have to come and go like this?''

''Don't worry. I'm always within five hundred feet.''

Megan looked at him from between her fingers. ''What do you mean you're always within five hundred feet?''

"If I'm not in my chosen container, I must always stay within five hundred feet of my master. And since the crock pot is gone, my only other alternative is to stay close to you."

Megan's hands dropped from her face. "The chosen container?"

"Once I spent three years in a tackle box. I didn't like that at all. Another time, I was trapped in a half-empty bottle of Dom Pérignon. Now that was fun."

"Five hundred feet?" Megan repeated as if trying to understand.

"That's right. I've got a five-hundred-foot leeway except when I'm in between masters. Then I can't leave the container of choice at all until someone lets me out. Of course, then, they become my master, and well, it's a vicious cycle."

Megan jumped up from the table and opened a cupboard. When she turned back to Gino, she had a plastic white container with a clear top. "Try this."

Gino shook his head. "That won't do."

"Listen, I know a Cool Whip container is a step down from your crock pot condo, but, for now, it'll have to do."

"You don't understand. I have to stay in the container my current master found me in."

"What is that? Part of the genie creed?"

"It prevents less scrupulous genies from playing hide and seek with their masters."

"Wait a minute." Megan began pulling out an endless variety of bowls and plates stacked high in the cupboard. "I must have something that'll work. What about this?'' She presented a large cranberry-colored bowl to Gino.

"Look.'' She picked up a matching cover and pressed it on the bowl. "It's got a patented lock-top.'' She lifted a corner of the cover, and the bowl burped at Gino.

He shook his head. "Nothing'll work but the crock pot.''

"You genies have a lot of rules.'' Megan began to put the dishes back into the cupboard. "Okay, tomorrow, we'll go to Wal-Mart and buy another crock pot.''

"That won't work, either.''

"Sure it will.'' Megan sat down at the table. "Listen, what size was your other one? Two and a half quarts? We'll buy you a five-quarter. You'll have double the room you had before.''

He shook his head. "It has to be the chosen container.''

"You mean the one you came in?''

He nodded.

"What if that container is gone? You and I are joined at the hip?''

"Give or take five hundred feet.''

"Well, blink or wriggle your nose or say *bibbidi-bobbideeboo* and bring it back.''

"I can't do that.''

"What do you mean you can't do that?''

"If you want me to bring it back, you have to wish for it.''

"You want me to make a wish for....a crock pot?''

He nodded again. "You're the keeper of the crock pot."

Megan dropped her head into her arms on the table. "Why is this happening to me?"

She heard an indignant snort. "You'd think you were the one cursed."

Megan raised her head. "Well, you're no help at all. The genie in *Aladdin* could do William Buckley. You couldn't even give me a simple Italian accent this afternoon."

"Lasciate ogni speranza, voi ch'entrate," he answered.

She eyed him. "What does that mean?"

"'Abandon all hope, ye who enter.' *La Señorita* is cranky."

Her smile came before she could stop it. "And what about the blood on the steering wheel?"

"At that time, my first concern was healing you. I would've steam-cleaned the whole car if you didn't shoo me away like I was still a fly."

"So, genies do have feelings?"

"Not normally. But, unfortunately, I'm one-third human. It's the other curse I carry."

"You're one-third human?"

"My father is King of the Ifrit Clan of the Jinn, but my mother was a mortal."

"Then, you're one-half human."

"Please." His laugh sounded, short and scornful. "One-third is penalty plenty. The blood of my genie ancestors is far superior to human. Human genes pale to half-power when the two are mixed."

Megan slowly looked him up and down. "So, what third of you is human?"

"The lowest common denominator," he answered without a trace of teasing. "My father's momentary descent to the mortal level is the burden I've carried since birth, rendering me impure and unworthy of the Royal Throne."

"Why?"

"Only a purebred genie can rule in the Upper Tier."

"But I thought you said after you granted my three wishes, the curse was over, and you'd be King."

"Yes." Gino smiled. "After I grant your three wishes, Ishtar has pledged to end both curses—the one she sentenced me with two thousand years ago and the eternal one willed me at birth by my mother's tainted heritage. Not only will I be free, I'll be pure, as pure as the air that created the angels." His gaze went past Megan to an unseen horizon. "Free of my mortal flaw, I will sit without shame on the throne now denied me."

Gino's gaze came back to Megan. "So, you want riches, power, everlasting youth, fine, but just because I'm your servant doesn't mean you have to treat me like, well, a servant."

"I didn't mean it, Gino. I just didn't know how to explain—"

He held up a halting hand. "And that name. Nowhere in the curse does it say I have to answer to…" He paused, took a deep breath, then spat out, "Gino.

I'm a genie prince, not an organ-grinder's trained monkey.''

Megan flattened her hands on the table. "How did you expect me to explain you to Kitty, never mind, the police? Don't you think my fiancé might wonder what I'm doing in the middle of a field with a man at midnight? Oh, wouldn't his mother have a field day with that one?"

"Doesn't your fiancé trust you?"

Megan's fingers clenched until the bones in the back of her hands became visible. "This isn't about Elliot and me. This is about you and me. Do you think this is fun? Since you've arrived, I've called the fire department out on a false alarm, lied to Elliot, been accused of drunk driving and wrecked my car. You may be a bona fide blue-blooded genie, buddy, but you can also be a royal pain in the..." She stopped and caught her own breath. She never, ever lost control like this.

The genie lifted one eyebrow. *"Deretano?"* he provided.

"What's that?"

"It's Italian for—"

"Never mind. I get the idea." She unfurled her fingers and waved her hand as if trying to brush away her anger. "I'm sorry." She massaged the spot between her eyebrows. "It's been a long day."

He leaned back in his chair, propping a foot on his knee. "You're tired."

"I am." Her eyes closed as she continued to knead

the bridge of her nose. "Anyway, we can't introduce you as Gilligan."

"It's Gilgamesh," he said, correcting her.

"Sorry, but that still won't play in Shady Hook, Connecticut."

"And Gino will?"

"It's better than Gilgamess."

"Gilgamesh." He corrected her once more.

Megan's fingers moved up to rub the middle of her forehead. "What would you like to be called?"

No one had ever asked him what he wanted before. He looked at her and saw once more the face he knew he'd never forget.

"I've always been partial to Elvis."

Megan's eyes opened. "Elvis?" She saw his earnest expression and checked her laughter.

She shrugged her shoulders. "I'll allow Elvis." She smiled. "But I draw the line at 'The King.'"

He smiled back. "Soon enough, I'll be called King."

"For now, we'll just say your mother was a big fan."

"My mother?" he questioned. "What does she have to do with this?"

"Nothing really. I was just saying—"

"We'll just stick with Gino."

"Are you sure?" Megan's voice was concerned. "It'd be easier, but we can explain Elvis."

"Gino will be fine."

"But—"

"I don't even know why we're discussing this."

He cut her off. "You're going to make your two last wishes, and I'll be gone."

Megan said nothing.

"You'll make your last two wishes, and I'll be gone?" His comment became a question.

She picked at a piece of metal trim pulling away from the table. Finally she met his eyes. "You can't expect me to just whip two wishes off the top of my head?"

"Yes, I can."

She lowered her gaze again. "I've got to think about it."

"What's to think about? There's money, power, thin thighs."

"Is that what your other masters wished for?"

"Pretty much. There was one woman's request involving the Flying Kamazov Brothers and twelve quarts of Ben & Jerry's Chunky Monkey, but that was an isolated incident."

He loved seeing the lines in her face lift and ease as she laughed. The thin creases across her brow smoothed, then disappeared.

He had to go to her. As certain as the fact he was her slave, he had no choice. He got up and kneeled before her. He took those tiny hands in his, covering the cuts, the red chapped skin at the knuckles.

"Megan." He spoke sincerely, her name tasting sweeter than rainwater on his tongue. "I can give you anything you want."

"Anything?" She moistened her lips. Her expression was rapt, her cheeks warming to the pink of the sunset-filled clouds.

"Yes." His answer came out a breath and a promise.

"But you can't give me more wishes?"

"Is that what you want?"

"No. I understand why masters are limited to three wishes, but what about love? Why can't you grant love?"

He shook his head. "It's beyond genie powers. We have no knowledge, no influence in that realm."

"What are you saying? Genies know nothing about love?"

Gino shrugged, his thumb absently stroking the back of her hand. "We mate frequently."

"So do humans."

"But I don't think that's what you mean by 'love.'"

"No, it's not," Megan agreed.

"Then, I'd have to say, you're right. We don't have love where I come from."

Megan looked at him in the careful way she had. He had seen her study him that way before. As if suddenly becoming conscious of the force of gravity, her features would fall, rendering her face a silent, thoughtful cameo.

"Sometimes, it's hard to find love where I come from, too," she said softly.

She stood up, taking her hands back from his. "I'm too tired to even think about all this right now. I've got to get some sleep. There's a bed in the spare room with clean sheets.''

Gino stood up, too. He hid his disappointment beneath a bland ''Thank you.''

Megan shifted her weight from foot to foot. ''Good night.''

''Good night...'' He almost said her name, but knew he only wanted to feel the touch of it on his lips once more. And for some reason, he felt that would be wrong.

She turned at the doorway, giving him a last glimpse of her face. ''We'll talk first thing in the morning, I promise,'' she said. ''Good night.''

Even in its fallen state, her face was still beautiful. ''Good night...'' He waited until he heard her bedroom door open and close. Then he allowed the name to fall as soft as satin on a woman's skin.

''Megan,'' he whispered.

Chapter Four

He could not sleep. Restlessness seized him, making his limbs twitch, his thoughts troublesome. He thought of turning into animal form, but abandoned the idea. There were not wings strong enough nor paws swift enough to carry him away from the sensations beating within his chest.

Two wishes were all that stood between him and his freedom. Two wishes, and he could return to the world from which he came, and triumphant, take his place on the throne as King.

Two wishes were all that was left of Ishtar's sentence.

Two wishes and a tiny woman.

Once more, he was tempted to soar high until the house he now stood in looked to be no more than a piece on a game board. But his yearnings were futile. At five hundred feet, he would fall back to the clay creatures, back to Megan.

So he stayed human, substituting mundane pacing around the room for flying close to the clouds. He made an endless circle around the tiny bedroom, finally stopping at the lone small window. The night was dark without a promise of the dawn.

His agitation should not surprise him. Its source was simple. Two thousand years he'd waited. Now so close, his patience could no longer be counted on. Even his reasoning seemed to have suffered, sending his head spinning at the mere presence of a woman— a human woman.

The moon was a silver sphere in the sky above. Two wishes, he thought. Two wishes, and then, he could go home.

His muscles threatened to go into spasms at their stillness. He made one, two, three turns around the bedroom, then stopped counting. Time seemed to stop. All he knew was the moon still reigned high when he headed toward Megan's room.

BENEATH A SINGLE SHEET, Megan watched the circle of the fan above. It turned leisurely, bringing a benign breeze to the woman with the wide-open eyes below. She tried to think of wishes but the possibilities were so overwhelming, her mind rebelled and went blank. Instead, against her brain's black tableau, appeared the man who had promised to make all her dreams come true.

Was he real? she had to ask once more. She couldn't deny what had happened at work today. The man obviously had powers past the realm of everyday ability.

Was that the reason her hands clenched and her

breath seemed to go faint every time she was in his presence?

Never, not with Elliot, not with any man or woman, had she felt such a greed to be with someone. That, more than the proof of genies and supernatural powers, scared her most of all.

The air stirred across her face as if it were a lover's touch. Two wishes, and he'd be gone. Life would be back to normal. She tried to focus on what she wanted, what she should ask him for.

Her mind saw only him.

Her bedroom door opened. She saw him in the shadows, wearing only loose white cotton pants gathered at the waist and ankle, and for a moment, she thought she'd dreamt him once more. Then, she realized she was not dreaming. Bronzed, bare-chested and beautiful, Gino stood in the dark doorway to her room.

She sat up, the sheet clenched to her own chest. "What're you doing in here? What do you want?"

"Don't be scared. I only want to show you something." He took a step toward the bed.

"I knew you were a pervert. Stay back."

He smiled, and even in the dim light, she saw the twinkle of amusement in his eyes.

"Come with me." He stepped closer to the bed. "I want to take you somewhere."

She pulled the sheet up tighter against her throat. "Where? To the Waramung Creek where you'll ravage my body, then drown me, leaving me to wash up on the bank with my eyes bulging and weeds tangled in my hair. No, thank you. I'm not leaving this world looking like one of those troll dolls they sell three for five dollars down at the Buck-a-rama."

She didn't really believe he'd harm her. Still, he was a tall, dark, too handsome man standing in the center of her hand-braided rag rug. Even if he meant no more than to show her how the moonlight crossed the kitchen, making the ordinary seem ethereal, he was in the end, bottom line, no doubts about it, dangerous.

His smile grew fuller, the light in his eyes brighter as if able to banish the darkness pervading the room.

"Take my hand." He was at the footboard, his arm extended, his fingers reaching for her.

"Trust me," he said.

She didn't even know if she could trust herself. His fingers curled slightly, beckoning to her. A thick, blue vein beat alongside his wrist where the skin stretched sheer.

She stared at that hand waiting for her and heard the words uttered so gently she'd had to lean forward to meet them.

Trust me.

Her fear receded. And hope, long banished, long denied, budded in her before she could stop it.

"Go ahead. Take my hand."

She'd stopped wanting so long ago, she'd thought she had no need left. She had agreed to marry Elliot, sacrificing her passion for the promise of life without pain. She didn't need shivers down her spine every second she was with her husband. She needed only one thing: security. Elliot would never leave her as her father had left her mother, broken in heart and spirit. Elliot would never abandon his children, rendering them bastards.

This man would.

This man and his magic promising her things she didn't dare to dream about.

She looked down at her own hands and saw they were smooth. Gone were the small cuts, the scars, the skin roughened by hard work. Slowly she unclenched one, holding it up to marvel. In the spaces between her fingers, she saw the face of the man at her footboard.

She smiled. He smiled back. Her healed hand went to his, feeling the warmth of his palm and the pulse of life in his veins.

"Close your eyes," he whispered.

She did as she was told.

When she opened them, she sat on a plain of sand and pebbles. Gino was beside her, still holding her hand. He muttered words she could not understand. The stony carpet beneath her became clothed with emerald green grass. It drew the eye to it and would have held it had it not been for the flowers and fruit trees springing from its lush soil.

Lilacs—white, lavender, deep purple—hung fat and full as if lulled by their own scent. Roses climbed upward, their delicate petals curled, laughing at the suddenly drab-looking clouds above them. Trees stood tall, sprouting their fruit without shame while feeding on the veins of the clearest water coursing through the ground.

"Oh!" The exclamation left Megan's mouth of its own accord as her gaze gathered in the colors and shapes surrounding her.

With her hand in his, Gino smiled as if happy she was pleased. His eyes closed for a second longer than the usual blink, and then before them, laid out by invisible hands on a square of fine linen, was a feast of fruits, meats, dates and breads. Cool wines in stoneware waited to be drunk.

"Try this." He urged toward her a biscuit spread with a thick, creamy paste.

She took it from his hand, the morsel sweet in her mouth, the touch of his fingertips still soft on hers.

Her eyes half closed with delight. "I've never tasted anything like it. What is it?"

"The cakes are called *kahks.* They're spread with *'ajameeyah,* which is butter, honey, a little flour and some spices. They are given as presents during the Minor Festival."

As he spoke, he poured a clear wine into a brass chalice. "Drink," he offered.

She shook her head. "I don't drink."

"As you wish."

He raised the cup to his own lips. Megan felt light-headed just watching him sip. He put the cup down, the pleasure of the wine evident on his lips. She was intoxicated, staring and smiling at him, how many seconds—five, ten, fifty—she didn't know. All she knew was the flowers paled beside his beauty.

"Come." He stood and offered his hand.

They walked hand in hand through a path just wide enough for two. The ground cover stayed a rich, surreal green, but the flowers became fewer until there were only trees larger and fuller than the ones they'd left behind.

The trees bore strange fruit. One bore berries as translucent as crystal, another entirely white. Circles of deep red clung to some boughs. Other limbs carried rounds of paler pink, yellow, blues of differing hues.

Megan dropped Gino's hand and went closer to the strange trees. She saw that the fruit were jewels—diamonds, pearls, sapphires, rubies. She reached up as if to touch them but did not.

Gino came up beside her and plucked a diamond, allowing it to catch the sunlight as he rolled it in his palm. He looked up from the sparkling jewel into her face.

"One wish. All these will be yours."

Comprehension came to Megan, closing something inside her that had just started to open like the flowers reaching toward the sun in the garden. The gems around her dulled and looked to her no more than colored rocks.

"So, money does grow on trees," she said flatly.

"It's all yours. Just say the word," Gino said luringly.

"Where would I wear them? To my annual bowling banquet at Eddie's Eats?"

"They're not only to wear." He held the diamond up. In his hand, its facets stayed full of heavenly light.

"They can bring great pleasure. You only have to wish for it."

"I see. You brought me out here to get me drunk and take advantage of me?" Her voice was joking, but she didn't smile. Gino's hand holding the diamond lowered.

"The last guy who tried this on me was the junior captain of the eighth-grade basketball team." Megan barely kept the light note in her tone. "Only he used a package of beef jerky and a stolen six-pack of Budweiser."

Gino's hand closed in a fist around the jewel. "Do not joke. I can give you great pleasure. I can bring you happiness. I can give you the world."

She looked into those eyes fiery with feeling and, at the moment, did not doubt him.

"Yet, you mock me."

"You may've improved the means, but your end is the same as that jock's hormone-inspired maneuvers."

Gino drew himself up, a dark, still relief against the sun. "Do you think I want you physically?"

"No, but you do want something from me I'm not ready to give yet."

"I offer you only a king's ransom." His hand opened, once more revealing the diamond. "Look. Have you ever seen such a jewel?"

Megan took the diamond from his palm. It lay cool and heavy in her own hand. "Yes."

"Where did you see such a treasure?" Gino scoffed.

"I met my father's mother once when I was very young. I remember she had the smoothest skin I'd even seen, and on her hand..." Megan raised the gem high, its perfect facets splintering her reflection. "She wore a ring with a jewel such as this."

"Your father is very rich?" Skepticism narrowed Gino's gaze.

"I imagine so." Her hand closed around the gem. "I never met him."

Megan saw, for the first time since he swirled out of her crock pot, that Gino did not know what to say.

"I only met his mother that one time. She came to our house and gave my mother and I a lot of money in an envelope. My mother tore it all up right in front of her. I remember the woman watching, her hand covering her mouth, that diamond so bright in the sun." Megan paused, her gaze no longer seeing her spectacular surroundings.

"My mother only spoke of that incident once before she died. What she said was that was the one and only time in her life money had brought her happiness."

There was another pause before Gino asked, his voice gentle, "Your mother is dead?"

Megan felt the hard weight of the diamond in her hand. "She ran off the road and hit a tree head-on. I was stretched out in the back seat, supposed to be asleep. The front seat cushioned my body. Mom was dead before the ambulance arrived. She was twenty-nine. I was thirteen."

Megan's gaze refocused, staring down at her closed

fist. She saw her hand smoothed by Gino's skill. This wasn't the hand that had touched her mother's lifeless body. That hand had been browned, textured like well-worn suede. Barely full-size, it had already boasted calluses on the pillows of its palms.

This hand was not hers. The skin was soft, fine-grained. The fingernails were polished and tinted pink, rivaling the opals hanging in nearby bunches. It was a stranger's hand.

Still she wanted it for her own. Perhaps, it was pure vanity; perhaps, it was the warm giddiness washing over her every time she looked at it, one simple glance transformed into a rare moment of feeling the starry-eyed schoolgirl. Perhaps, every time she used this hand to touch, hold, reach, release, she'd remember when it took another's hand in complete and total trust. She'd remember a moment when it had been easy to believe in frolicking among fluffy white clouds and strolling through a garden orchard of gems.

She looked down at the hand hiding the diamond, and the moment dulled and was gone. She felt properly foolish.

She gave Gino the jewel, saying, "I don't know what I want, but, as soon as I do, I'll let you know. In the meantime, don't waste your sweet cakes and sparkling gems on me."

She suffered his study, keeping her face as expressionless as her voice. At first, so lightly she wondered if she imagined it, then gradually, with greater force, she felt the ground beneath them tremble. She looked down as the brilliant grass turned back to dusty dirt, then mere air.

"Give me your hand," Gino commanded.

She did as he asked, giving him the hand he'd given to her.

"Close your eyes," he ordered.

She did, the very boundaries of her body seeming to dissolve. She floated for a moment somewhere between heaven and earth, her hand in Gino's her sole anchor. Then, once more, there was only darkness.

Careful not to wake her, Gino returned her to her bed. When he released her hand, she turned onto her side, curling into a ball. He looked down at her profile, her features now calm with the cloth of sleep.

All the females he'd taken to the garden had succumbed easily to the intoxicating perfume of the flowers, the seductive sweetness of the wine, the trees heavy with their temptations. The wishes had been made swiftly, one, two, three, and he'd gone on to another master before morning.

But, perhaps, those women had not suffered so much as this one. Perhaps, the others had found their happiness easily, effortlessly.

This woman wasn't to be so easy. His hand brushed back a wisp of hair that had fallen across her cheek. The gloss of her skin surpassed the gem he still held wrapped tightly in his hand.

This Megan, she was different from the other creatures of clay. He should feel disappointment, frustration, impatience, but those weren't the emotions that came.

No, this wasn't going to be easy. Not for her...not for him.

MEGAN WOKE to the morning sun, but not even the strong light could banish what had happened during the night. She remembered every moment, each detail and knew it hadn't been a dream. She relived the sight, taste, touch of the night before, seeing the garden to rival Eden, the gems arching the slender boughs that had held them. She remembered her awe...and her anger now soothed by slumber.

She saw Gino's face, at first, so pleased by all he'd created. She saw his expression become startled, confused, and ultimately, insulted when she spurned his offerings. Yet, when she spoke of her mother's death, if he'd pitied her, he'd been sensitive enough to conceal it.

She could allow his presumption she could be wooed by riches. She was sure material wealth had been at the top of many other masters' lists. It might have made her top three, too, if she'd not seen at such a young age, how money can buy as much pain as pleasure.

No, she didn't need millions, and she didn't need Gino feeling sorry for her. She'd done just fine before he showed up; she'd do just as well after he was gone. She didn't need his magic. She was going to marry Elliot, and together, they would work and save and spend their money practically and wisely. They would never be wealthy. Elliot liked to claim they would be, especially after two gin and tonics, but Megan didn't want money. She only wanted to know when she woke up in the morning, there was a roof over her head, food in the refrigerator and a father for her children. It wasn't such a greedy dream.

It certainly didn't need the hocus-pocus of a smug, overbearing, irritating know-it-all puff of smoke who had done nothing but disrupt her life since he'd arrived.

All she had to do was make two wishes, and all her problems—and his—would be solved.

So, what did she want?

It wasn't material wealth. He'd said jewels could bring her pleasure, but she knew it was a pale pleasure. She'd learned long ago such a richer joy could be had by simply looking out her bedroom window to the full bloom of flowers across her backyard. There, she'd planted a spring overture of daffodils and tulips, a summer symphony of roses and irises, an autumn sonata of mums sheltered by a six-foot golden glow.

Suddenly yearning to see the current kaleidoscope of her garden, Megan sat up and stretched away the last remnants of sleep. She walked barefoot to the window to see where the coneflowers boasted their violet blooms, and the hibiscus stood like soldiers, their scarlet red flowers envying the lilies of the valley dancing delicately below in the warm summer wind.

Megan opened the white muslin curtains, already smiling at the thought of her backyard border. She looked. Her eyes went wide.

She saw water—not the nearby Candlewood Lake or the larger Saugatuck Reservoir, but the sea, acres and acres of a watery plain, stretching out until it sliced the sun beginning its journey upward. There was sand, white and as fine as sugar and a smell of watery life and death so strong and crisp it stung the nostrils.

Not moving from the window, Megan yelled a single summons. A circle of seagulls stopped their picking in the sand and looked her way. She yelled again and the birds lifted, leaving the land for the safer ceiling of the sky.

One name sounded across the deserted beach and through the one-story house:

"Gino!"

There was no answer.

Megan strode out of the bedroom and down the hall, opening closed doors and looking in the rooms right and left. She got to the kitchen just as he came in. His arms were full of deep-colored fruit.

"I've got breakfast." He offered the basket. "The mangoes are extraordinary here."

She walked toward him until there was only the barrier of the basket between them. "Where is here?"

He set the basket down on the table. "Somewhere south of the equator." He sat down and began to peel a thick-skinned guava, exposing its deep pink inners.

She braced her arms on the table. "Why?"

"Your own deserted private island. The man of your dreams." His shoulders did a little shimmy. "Isn't it every woman's fantasy?"

"Another paradise, Gino?"

"Your paradise." He looked up at her through a veil of black lashes. "If you wish."

She sat down at the table as if she were a suddenly deflated balloon. "I asked you to take me home last night. Didn't you listen?"

"I listened and understood completely." He popped a chunk of fruit into his mouth. "There are no modern conveniences here. No sixty-inch screen TVs, no call-waiting, no megamalls, no microwave popcorn. The people are poor here, but they're happy. They have the sea to bathe their bodies, the sun to dry their skin, the land to feed them fruits. They barter their talents for the services they need and when they work, they sing the most happy songs."

"This is what you think I want?"

A slice of guava stopped midway to Gino's mouth. "It's not?"

Megan looked down at an oblong mango. She touched the orange color bursting across the perfect curve of its skin. "No."

The salmon-colored fruit that was balanced on the blade of Gino's knife began to tremble. "What do you want then?"

Megan picked up the orange fruit. "Right now..." She bit into the mango's firm flesh. She chewed hard. "I want to go home."

Gino set down his knife. "Why?"

She didn't know how to explain. She didn't know what she wanted, but she knew it wasn't a primitive island miles away from the small community where she'd lived, worked and learned to thrive. Her ramshackle house, bought with the small life insurance policy her mother had left her, was the first real home Megan had ever had. Funny, her mother had always wanted to give her a home of her own. In the end, she had.

"It's Sunday. I've laundry" was all Megan told Gino.

"I give you paradise, and you're worried about the wash?"

Megan took another bite. "I can't go to work tomorrow in my underwear."

"You don't have to go to work at all. You can lay on the beach and sun in the nude all day."

Megan shook her head as she took another bite. "Skin cancer," she said, her mouth full of yellow-red fruit.

"You can sit in the shade and drink papaya juice and dream."

"I can do that in Connecticut."

"When? During the spin cycle?" Gino set down his knife. "You know what your problem is? You're no fun."

Megan's mouth opened. A trickle of juice rolled from the corner of her lips to her chin. "I'm fun."

His hands flapped the air once, dismissing her statement. He stood up and went to the window, looking out to the sea. "I can make you paint like Picasso."

"I'd rather paint like Megan Kelly," she told his back.

"I can make you sing like a nightingale, dance like a spirit."

"If I want to sing, I just open my mouth." He heard the scrape of a chair, her voice coming closer to him.

"If I want to dance, I just spread out my arms like this."

He turned to find her in front of him, her feet repeating a graceful pattern, her hips swaying to invisible sound. Her head tilted back, exposing a length of long, smooth throat. Her raised arms formed an arc as her small, slender body moved like the waves outside the window.

She spun around once in a lazy circle, the thin, cotton gown she wore billowing. The tiny-flowered material settled as her spin stopped, allowing a sway to show the curve of a hip, a breast, the flat, hard angle of ribs, only suggesting the body that lay beneath the faded fabric.

She took a step toward him, her lids lowered to half-mast, her arms moving closer together, inviting him in. He hesitated, in that second, wondering once more where this ordinary woman gained her power.

He took her newly healed hands in his, and their bodies came together, his hips and belly finding softer, smaller mates. He felt the gentle push of her breasts against his chest, and his throat felt as if it were filled with cotton batting. He could not swallow.

"I haven't danced in so long," he heard her murmur.

He looked down. The crest of her cheek lightly

rested on the round of his shoulder. Her eyes had closed. The curve of her mouth was of a child's smiling in her sleep.

"You see..." He felt the movement of her mouth against his collarbone. "Paradise isn't found in bulging bank accounts or faraway lands." She lifted her head, her gaze fixing on him. "Do you understand?"

He did not so he said nothing.

"It's right here." Her hand lifted and laid against his chest. "Inside you." Her hand went to her own breast. "Inside me."

Gino's voice was thick. "What can I give you then?"

Her answering gaze stayed solemn. "When I know, I'll tell you."

Her head dropped. Their steps slowed.

"I only know it's not diamonds or deserted beaches or dancing different from this right now." She stopped moving. "Can't you understand?"

In her somber study, he saw her plea that he understand.

"Nothing easy," he half asked, half answered.

Her neck muscles relaxed, and her head settled against his shoulder, confirming what he'd just said, what he'd already realized the night before. They began dancing again.

"It's easy for you, Gino, isn't it? You know what you want," she said, the breath of her words warming the silk of his shirt.

"Yes." His reply was automatic. The muscles of his body stiffened involuntarily.

Her head came up, spilling her hair behind her shoulders. Her eyes regarded him, challenging him to say it.

"I want to be King." All the slur had left his voice.

Her eyes studied him. Their hips continued to swing, their shoulders to ripple. "Is that all you've ever wanted?"

"There is nothing else," he replied.

"So, all that stands between you and your happiness is me?"

He eased her into the center of the kitchen. He gave her question the same sidestep, even though they both knew it was the truth. "What'll make you happy, Megan Kelly?"

Her head returned to the square of his shirt, hiding her expression. She said nothing. Against the horizontal plane that held his heart, he felt a half shrug of her shoulders as if they were too heavy to lift more than that.

They swayed in silence. He tilted his head to the right, and her hair, as soft as rain, skimmed beneath the hard edge of his jaw. The smell of wet sand and sultry air was replaced by a sweetness only possible when a woman was so near.

"Gino?"

Lulled by the slow steps and the lovely feel of her body against him, he'd closed his eyes. Bound by this woman in a perfectly comfortable blackness neither here nor there, he answered with a sleepy, "Mmm?"

He felt her head leave his shoulder. The spot where she'd laid it stayed warm.

"I'm happy now."

He opened his eyes to hers. Their green had deepened to forest, the pupils opening into a darkness a man could drown in.

He said nothing, not trusting his voice, which once more seemed strangled. When he didn't respond, her head nestled against him again, her eyes covered, no longer asking for an answer.

He looked down to the ringlets that looked as if they were spun silk, his lips wishing to lay on their feathery bed.

He didn't understand. She wasn't a goddess, a sorceress, an angel, a witch. She was a small, simple woman, ordinary in every respect.

Except she could open her arms and cast magic far greater than his own legendary powers. She smiled and he was under her spell.

"You're a strange creature, Megan Kelly," he said.

He heard her laugh before she even raised her head. "Now there's the pot calling the kettle black."

He joined her laughter and the tightness in his chest lessened, making it easier to breathe.

They were still swaying, still smiling silently when she said, "Let's go home, Gino."

He nodded. He had no choice. Her every wish was his command.

Chapter Five

She was back in her own bed. The sun was still shining. But by now, she was no longer sure if she was dreaming or awake, home or hurling headlong through the universe.

She wasn't sure of anything at this moment.

She sat up as she met the memory of Gino's hand on her skin. The exotic incense surrounding him like an opiate still filled her nostrils. She knew the beat of his heart, which had quickened when she nestled against his chest.

It was the same beat that had begun within her own body. Her feet had moved to it. The pulse of her blood had echoed it. She placed her hand against her chest and knew the rhythm once more, weaker but there nonetheless.

At that moment, it was the only reality she knew.

She swung her legs out of the bed and walked to the window, welcoming the cool shock of tile against her bare feet. She pushed back the curtains. Her flowers, pink, purple, coral, cream, welcomed her home. Her sigh was audible.

"Me-e-e-e-gan," Gino called. "Come here. I've got a surprise for you."

Oh, no! What now?

She slipped on a robe and walked in the direction of Gino's off-key singing. She stopped right before the entrance to the kitchen, afraid to look.

"I see your shadow. Come on in," Gino said. "There's nothing to be afraid of."

"Would you put that in writing, please?" Megan peeked around the corner of the doorway. A silver tray of pastries covered the center of the table. A crystal bowl of fruit rose behind it. A covered chafing dish stood on the counter. Coffee perked patiently beside it.

Megan stepped into the room, a smile spreading across her lips.

In black tie, Gino stood beside the refrigerator. He acknowledged Megan's pleasure with a smile of his own before bowing low. "Madam, breakfast is served."

Megan walked to the counter and lifted the cover of the chafing dish. In its belly, paper-thin crepes swam in an orange-scented sea. Still smiling, she turned to Gino. "Did you cook these yourself?"

He rolled his eyes. "What do you think?"

Megan laughed half at herself, half in pure pleasure. She sat down, eyeing the mound of pastries. "I guess there are some advantages to having you around." She reached for a flaky square dusted with powdered sugar.

Gino went to the counter and poured them each a

cup of coffee into white china cups edged in gold. "I figured after the night you had, you'd be starving."

"I am." The pastry was midway to Megan's mouth.

Gino stirred his coffee. "You must've been more tired than hungry, though, if you were able to sleep this late."

"Late? What time is it?" Her gaze shifted to the wall clock. The pastry fell to the table uneaten. "Oh, no!" She jumped up, knocking over her chair, and ran from the room.

"What's the problem?" Gino had followed her into her bedroom, a cup of coffee in each hand. He placed one on the dresser where Megan was opening drawers and flinging out clothes. He took a long sip from the other one as he settled in the chair in the corner.

"It's 1:25!" Megan slammed closed one drawer and opened another below it.

Gino took another unhurried sip of his coffee. "Yes?"

"Elliot and I are supposed to be at his mother's at two. He'll be here any minute." She suddenly froze. "Did you hear a car door?" she whispered.

Before Gino could answer, there was the sound of steps coming up the back sidewalk. Alarm lit up Megan's features.

"It's Elliot. Get rid of that breakfast!"

"But you didn't even eat yet," Gino observed.

"Get…" Megan's voice rose, then just as quickly dropped to a hiss, "rid of it now!"

With maddening precision, Gino set his coffee on

the saucer balanced on his thigh, closed his eyes for not longer than three pounding beats of Megan's heart, then opened them, picked up his cup and took another sip.

"It's gone?" Megan heard the slam of the back screen door.

Gino calmly nodded, sipping his coffee.

"*Me-e-e-e-gan,*" Elliot called.

"Now you go," Megan ordered Gino in a frantic whisper.

"*Me-e-e-e-gan?*" Elliot called again.

Gino sipped his coffee.

"I'll be right out," Megan yelled. She ran into the small adjoining bathroom and turned on the water. She ran back into the bedroom. "I'm in the shower," she yelled, glaring at Gino. He smiled pleasantly back at her.

"Your coffee's getting cold," he said.

"You're in the shower?" Elliot's voice was closer.

Megan tiptoed toward the door. Holding her breath, she slowly, soundlessly locked it. She tiptoed back to the center of the room. With her features in a tense pose, she pointed at Gino, then pointed at the window.

"You're not even dressed yet?" Elliot called from the other side of the door. "It's after one-thirty."

Megan watched the doorknob turn one way, then the other. Her gaze shot back to Gino. Her outstretched finger stabbed toward the window.

"I overslept."

"You overslept?" The knob stopped turning. "You never oversleep."

"After working all those extra hours, then the accident, I must've slept right through the alarm. I'll be out in a minute." The room was starting to steam up.

Even behind the closed door, Megan could hear Elliot's cluck of disapproval. "I better go call Mom and tell her we'll be late. She isn't going to like this."

Megan didn't move until she heard Elliot's footsteps heading toward the kitchen.

"Great," she mumbled as she moved back to the dresser. She pulled a cotton shirt from the drawer, considered it a moment, then dropped it beside the other clothes strewn on the floor.

"I guess I better change, too," Gino said. "I'm a little overdressed for the occasion."

Megan turned back to him. He was now in pressed linen trousers and a white button-down shirt, rolled up at the sleeves.

"You're not going."

Gino looked down at his outfit. "You don't like this? I thought it was suitable for an afternoon of sucking down brewskis and swearing at the sports channel. I imagine that's what Elliot does while you gals cook him dinner, serve it to him, clean up after him."

"I don't care if you go naked—"

"Do you think Elliot's mother would prefer that?"

"Because you're not going."

"Here's my second surprise for you today—yes, I am."

"I can't believe ten minutes ago I actually said there were advantages to having you around."

"Listen, I'm not exactly overjoyed about spending the next few hours listening to the wit and wisdom of Elliot and his mom, but you—" He pointed his finger at her. "Threw away the crock pot."

"I didn't throw it out...exactly," Megan attempted to defend herself.

"The bottom line is it's not here. Which means you're stuck with me for now. Do you think you could turn that water off?" He smoothed the legs of his trousers. "My creases are beginning to fade."

She went to the bathroom and turned off the shower.

"*Me-e-e-e-gan,* are you dressed?" Elliot's footsteps came down the hall and stopped outside the door.

Megan looked at Gino, putting a finger to her lips. "Almost ready."

"Were you talking to me a moment ago?" Elliot asked from the other side of the door. "I thought I heard voices again."

"I was singing in the shower."

"Singing in the shower," Elliot grumbled as he walked back down the hall. "Shake a leg. Mom already put the roast in, and I don't like it well-done." The sound of a television program started.

Megan moved toward the closet. "What am I going to wear?" She considered a high-necked white blouse, a striped shirtdress, a pair of black pants, then abandoned them to the other end of the metal rod. "I wish I had..."

"Yes?"

She looked back at Gino. He was sitting up straight, an eager look in his eyes.

"What I meant to say was I need something to wear."

Gino slumped back in his chair. Megan shoved aside a few empty hangers, coming to a paisley blouse.

"How 'bout this?" Gino asked.

Megan turned to face him, almost toppling over in the spiked heels she was now wearing. She steadied herself on the bed, straightening slowly as her gaze came up her legs in black leather pants, her midriff bared by a black lace bustier. She let go of the bedpost, looking up from fingernails, now three inches long and painted red.

"You forgot the dog collar," she said.

"At least, I didn't pierce your belly button."

"I appreciate your thoughtfulness."

"Just trying to help out."

"If I show up like this for dinner and put Elliot's mom into cardiac arrest, it wouldn't exactly have a positive effect on our already shaky relationship."

"Point taken. Okay, something a little less heart-stopping. How's this?"

Megan was afraid to look. When she did, gone were the leather and lace. In their place was a plaid-pleated skirt that touched her knee, a white turtleneck and a navy blue blazer with an embroidered crest on the pocket.

She looked up at Gino. "You're having a good time, aren't you?"

He smiled his answer.

Megan looked down at her penny loafers. "I've heard some guys go for the schoolgirl look but I don't know about their mothers."

Gino stood up. "I'm just trying to show you you're being a little silly. What's the big deal anyway?"

Megan let out a nervous laugh. "You've never met Elliot's mother. Every time she looks at me, I feel like my shirt is buttoned the wrong way or I forgot to zipper my pants."

"You've nothing to worry about, Megan. You're a beautiful woman. Look."

Megan didn't move. Had he really said she was beautiful?

"Look in the mirror," he commanded.

Her feet moved to the tone in his voice. She wiped away the steam that had settled on the bureau mirror and slowly revealed a woman in a strapless, pearl-beaded sheath, exposing skin so creamy it was hard to tell where the dress ended and the flesh began.

Her lips, painted pale cranberry, formed an O. The rest of the face was hers, too. It was the face of an extraordinarily beautiful woman.

"How...?"

"It was easy." Gino's image joined hers as he came up behind her. "The beauty was always there. I just added a few enhancements."

He put his hands on her shoulders and his head close to hers where her hair had been piled into an artless crown of curls. He spoke into her ear, his breath stirring a wayward tendril. "Elliot's mom, eat your heart out."

It wasn't vanity that kept Megan before the mirror unable to move. It wasn't amazement that parted her lips with an endless breath. It was the presence of Gino beside her, the picture of them together, the look in his eye, the longing in her heart.

"*Me-e-e-e-gan!*" Elliot yelled. "We've got to go."

Megan's eyes lost their dreamy look. "Could you give me something a little less Bob Mackie?"

"Yes, it's a little dramatic for day-wear." Gino lifted her chin with a strong tapered finger. "But this afternoon when Elliot's mom looks at you like your blouse is on backward, you remember this image. And you remember, I'm nearby."

Megan turned around, seeing only his beauty now. "Where will you be? In the sky, in the house, in the car trunk?"

"Don't worry. I'll be around."

"*Me-e-ee-e-gan!*" Elliot's voice was loud and exasperated.

"You better go," Gino advised.

"What form will you be in? Land, animal or mineral? I don't like this at all."

"Go." Gino took her by the shoulders and pushed her toward the door.

She took two steps forward, then stopped. She looked back at Gino. "But—"

Elliot began to pound on the door. "*Me-e-e-e-gan!*"

She looked back at the door.

''Go!'' Gino whispered behind her. He gave her a pat on her rear end.

She turned, indignation coming on the heels of her surprise. He was gone. All she saw was her own reflection in the mirror. Her hair was still carelessly tousled, her features perfected by the expert touch of makeup, but she now wore a peach-colored dress of the softest silk. Its neck was scooped, the material forming against her breasts in a demure curve, then falling into a long length of skirt that swirled about her legs to just around the ankle. For the first time in her life, she felt like a fairy-tale princess.

One moment, one man, and her life had changed, been altered forever. She walked to the door and opened it, all the while, giving thanks, silent and strong.

GINO SWUNG FORWARD and back, side to side. He was trying to shake off the ladybug tickling him as she made her way up his left lacy frond. He was also trying to get a better view of Megan seated below on the wicker couch. There she was. She looked spectacular. She leaned toward the coffee table, and his view was blocked by Elliot sitting beside her. He hoped she wasn't going to peek beneath her cocktail napkin again. He twisted to the left to get a better view. Some water from the bottom of the plastic planter sloshed out over the side.

Elliot's mother patted the tight bulge of her French twist. ''Are we supposed to get rain this afternoon?''

Elliot turned to his mother, then looked beyond her

to the cloudless summer sky showing through the screened porch walls. Past the jut of Elliot's Adam's apple, Gino saw Megan holding high her glass, peering up through its bottom.

"I don't think the weatherman called for rain?" Elliot said. "Do you, Megan?"

Megan looked at Elliot and his mother from behind the amber filter of her glass now two inches from her nose. She quickly set her drink down. "Anything's possible."

"Is there something wrong with your iced tea?" Elliot's mother asked.

"No, not at all." Megan took a large gulp. "Mmm, delicious. Is this freshly brewed?"

Get a grip, girl, Gino thought. The macramé hanger holding the plastic planter slowly turned him away from Megan. He heard Elliot's mother say, "Of course. Is it strong enough or, perhaps, you prefer something stronger?"

"Something stronger?" Megan sounded confused. The planter completed its revolution until Gino faced Megan once more. She was shredding her cocktail napkin.

"I've got wine," Elliot's mother said, "and I think there's still a bottle of whiskey around here somewhere that Mr. Barford, God rest his soul, liked to take a nip from now and again when he thought I wasn't looking."

Living with this broad, I bet Mr. Barford took a lot of nips, Gino thought as the planter started to turn again.

"I don't drink, Dolores."

"No? You're not just saying that for my benefit, are you, dear?"

Hello, Elliot, did you go to sleep? I don't care if she did give birth to your hairless butt, your mother is crucifying our gal here. And will you stop that? Gino snarled up at the beaded, macramé hanger as it twisted to the left. *I'm getting dizzy.*

The plant hanger stopped moving. And Elliot, as if he'd also heard Gino's thoughts, said, "The Breathalyzer test Megan took was completely negative."

Gino set the plant hanger back in motion, spinning until Elliot came back into sight. Elliot's mother and Megan were also staring at the man in stupefaction.

"Breathalyzer test?" Dolores questioned. Her gaze moved to Megan.

She's going to marry this pork chop? Gino wondered. His fronds shook with disbelief.

Megan's features were frozen like an animal caught in the headlights. "It's really quite amusing," she said.

"Amuse me then," Dolores said. Her face had a shiny, brittle look.

"It's not like it sounds," Elliot explained. "Megan was coming home late last night—"

"From work," Megan quickly added.

Elliot nodded. "Right. From work, and she ran off the road, nothing serious, thank goodness, my girl here is still all in one piece," he said in one big breath. He patted Megan's hand, which was clenching the shredded napkin. She gave him a halfhearted smile. "And the police gave Megan a Breathalyzer test."

Between tight lips, Dolores uttered one word: "Why?"

Now Elliot had the frozen-fear look on his face. He turned to Megan. "Why?" he said, his tone indicating the question hadn't occurred to him before.

Oh, my Megan, I mean, my master. Gino quickly corrected himself. The pot moved in a sympathetic sway. He had never gotten personally involved with his masters. In his line, it would only complicate matters, and frankly, he'd never been drawn that way toward the others. Maybe he was getting sentimental in his old age; maybe it was because Megan was his last master. Maybe it was the way her hands, knotted in her lap, looked so small and delicate. Maybe it was all those things and more that made him want to transform into human shape and take her by those tiny hands away from Elliot and his hideous mother.

But it wouldn't be the right thing—not for Megan, not for him. He was already too involved, and as he knew from his father's example, a partnership between humans and his kind only brought pain. He could give Megan two more wishes. And nothing else.

So, he stayed in vegetation shape. The pot swung slowly side to side, and Gino waited, like Elliot and his mother, for Megan's answer.

"I'm sure it's standard procedure." Megan took a sip of her iced tea. When she swallowed, she made a short, strangled sound.

"Standard?" Dolores interrogated. "To accuse someone of drunk driving? There must have been a reason."

"It was Saturday night," Elliot rationalized.

"Yes, and I'd been weaving down the road for..." Megan's voice went low as she listened to her words. "About a mile," she finished saying quietly. "I was very tired."

Elliot's mother stared at her, unconvinced.

"I'd worked three shifts in two days."

"That damn factory," Elliot muttered. "It'll kill us all."

"It provided a roof over our heads and food on the table for seventeen years," his mother noted.

"Until it sent Pop to an early grave."

"No, until you got out of the army and took your father's place on the floor. Crelco's been good to this family. Already you're a manager," Elliot's mother said pointedly.

"No, Mom, I'm in waste management. It's not quite the same. But don't worry. I'm not going to end up like Pop, dead at forty-three from working sixty-five hours a week. And what about you? Thirty-two years of service at the garment mill."

"O'Reilly's treated me well."

"Until the arthritis you got from sewing their damn stretch pants prevented you from keeping up. Then what'd you get? A cake, six months unemployment and two hands that hurt you so bad, you can't tie your apron on in the morning."

Elliot let go of Megan's hand and reached for his

mother's, gently pulling them out from beneath the folds of her dress where she always hid them.

He took the curled, misshapen fingers in his. "That's not going to happen to me...or my wife. We'll all live here, at first, but it won't be long, I promise. We'll all move to a bigger house, a Colonial with real brick steps and maybe one of those little huts you always talked about, what were they called, Mom?"

Elliot's mom indulged him with a smile. "A gazebo."

Elliot released his mother's hands and sat back against the couch cushions, his arms spread like wings along its pillowed back. "A gazebo," he said to the air, the word sounding like an incantation as it rolled off his tongue.

Dolores stood up, her hands returning to the soft pleats of her skirt. "I'd better check the roast. Elliot hates it well-done," she confided to Megan. She patted her son's head as she passed him.

"What would you like in your house, Megan?" Elliot smiled, still caught in the spirit of his imagination. "A marble fireplace in the bedroom? A walk-in closet? A bathroom with a whirlpool tub and one of those separate French toilets?"

Megan wriggled a smile, but she didn't speak until after the back door closed and Dolores went into the house.

"Elliot?"

"Mmm?" he answered from somewhere in his fantasy.

She put her hand on his arm, trying to get his attention. "Your mother? She's going to live with us?"

The back door opened, and Dolores sailed into the small, screened room. "Won't be but a few minutes longer. I was able to save the roast. No small feat, considering how late you were." She looked at Megan with direct disapproval.

From above, Gino rustled his leaves indignantly. He'd slain two-headed beasts, brought one-eyed giants to their knees, wrestled with fire-breathing gargoyles and emerged the victor. But how did one deal with a sharp-tongued mother-in-law?

"Elliot," his mother said as she reached up to Gino's pot. "Did I tell you Harriet's daughter is back for a visit?" She poked her fingers into Gino's soil.

Hey, lady, you don't know me that well.

"No, you didn't mention it, Mom."

"She just completed her residency at Mount Sinai. Such a brilliant girl. She asked about you, of course." The older woman pulled off several yellowed leaves.

Watch it! Those are still attached, you know.

Dolores turned away from the fern. "She was crushed when I told her you were engaged."

She started to sit down, but not before Gino shifted his weight, tilting the pot so a stream of water fell, forming a small pool onto the seat cushion. Dolores sat down, then shot up.

"Mom, what's wrong?" Elliot stood up, immediately at her side.

"This seat!" She turned around and looked down. "It's soaked."

"Are you sure it's not still damp from the night air?" Elliot felt the cushion. "Did it rain early this morning? Maybe we have a leak in the roof. Take my seat."

Dolores settled in next to Megan who was intently checking out each corner of the ceiling.

"I better take a quick look at the roof." Elliot started toward the side door.

"It's almost time to eat," his mother protested.

"It'll only take a minute." He was gone.

Megan's gaze dropped from the ceiling to Elliot's mother. She fashioned a smile.

Dolores half smiled back. Megan folded her hands in her lap. Dolores's were knotted beneath the folds of her dress.

"Kimberly, Harriet's daughter, was Elliot's girlfriend for years and years, but then, he probably told you all about that."

Megan kept smiling that silly smile.

"You probably even know her. Tall girl with long, blond hair, homecoming queen, class president, class valedictorian. Wait a minute. I have her and Elliot's picture when they were crowned the royal couple at the senior prom."

The overly bright smile stayed on Megan's face until Dolores left the room. Then, Gino saw it slip away, leaving only sadness on his master's face. His carefully reasoned objectivity fell away just as quickly.

"Here it is." Dolores came back into the room, carrying a gilt-framed photo. "Aren't they a beautiful couple? Everyone thought they'd be married," she was saying when there was a knock at the front door.

Dolores looked up. "Who could that be? Here, hold this." She handed Megan the picture as she stood up.

Megan stared at the attractive couple in her hands—Elliot, his handsomeness tempered with the softness of youth; Kimberly, as delicately bloomed as a white magnolia. They smiled forever, rhinestone crowns perched on their heads, wholly the center of their own universe.

Megan had left school at sixteen to support herself. She'd earned her general equivalency diploma nights at the community college. There'd been no proms, no homecomings, no senior skip days, no such lovely foolishness. But she had worn a dress like this once, and she had stood with a man and looked as blissfully, invulnerably happy. It had been just this afternoon in her very own bedroom with Gino by her side.

From inside the house, came a shriek, followed by the theme from the "Phantom of the Opera." Megan rushed into the house, leaving Elliot and Kimberly behind.

From the front hall, she heard Elliot's mother ask, "What're you doing? Stop that!" The overture was reaching its height of power.

Megan rounded the staircase, first only seeing the back of Dolores as she stood in the foyer, still holding the front door open. "You can't do that in here, young man," she was saying.

Megan maneuvered a few steps closer until she

could see over Dolores's tall shoulder. In the past twenty-four hours, she'd thought nothing could surprise her anymore.

She was wrong.

In the middle of the living room's red shag rug, a man stood, now shimmying, now bumping and grinding in a full-length black satin cape and white half-mask. And almost nothing else.

Megan moved past Dolores until she stood in front of her. "What do you think you're doing?"

The man winked at her with his one unmasked eye. The music quieted, rendering the room a restful interlude. The cape slipped from the man's shoulders, and like the music, the women became quiet.

He came toward them, pure physical form unfettered. Pride carried the strong, sculpted line of his shoulders, the rise of his rib cage, the lean length of his torso. Strength was in each step of his muscled thighs, each pulsing curve of his calves. He passed Megan, so close his ambergris air washed over her, barely touching her before moving on, making her yearn for more of his sweet scent.

She wanted to fill her every sense with him, gaze on his physical form until her eyes watered with the pure unreal beauty of him. She ached to touch the smooth, brown length of his skin, to know where it stretched firm over muscle, where it loosened and became soft and vulnerable.

She could almost taste him now, a mixture of rich, exotic flavors, spicy on the tongue so the taste lingered. Hours later, she would only have to lick her lips to feel his full flavor inside her.

She tried to close her eyes as he passed, afraid her need would be naked in her eyes, but the darkness, coupled with the erotic perfume of him, made her dizzy. She opened her eyes.

This was desire. It had destroyed men, brought countries to war, toppled thrones.

And now Megan knew why.

The half-masked man took Dolores's hand from beneath its cover of cloth and led her to the center of the room. A tango began on the portable stereo in the corner. He uncovered her other hand and swung her into his arms, pulling her tight against his body and bringing his cheek to hers.

They began to dance, Elliot's mother, at first, stiff, awkward, reluctant; the man, soothing, patient, staring into her eyes until her steps matched his and her body stayed tight against his even when he loosened his hold.

"What the hell is going on here?"

Both women had completely forgotten about Elliot until now. He stood behind Megan, his face a mottled red color. His mother and Megan turned to him. The music stopped.

"Who the hell is that? Where the hell did he go?"

Megan and Dolores turned back to see that Elliot was right. The man had disappeared.

"Elliot, stop swearing," his mother said, her cheeks still a young girl's pink. "It was just some sort of singing telegram, I believe." She looked at

Megan for confirmation. "He must have run out the back. You probably scared the pants off him."

"His pants were already off him, Mom."

Dolores sat down in a vinyl La-Z-Boy and fanned her face with her hands. "It was obviously a prank. The girls in my bridge club must have put him up to it. Or maybe he was at the wrong house." Her head fell back against the swell of the chair. She smiled up at the ceiling. "Who knows?"

"Mom?"

"What, Elliot?" She was becoming annoyed.

"Your hands," he answered in amazement.

He walked toward her. She looked down and wriggled fingers, once gnarled and twisted, now completely flexible. She squeezed them into fast little knots, then stretched them until the lines across the palm pulled tight. Her hands took Elliot's and held them tight.

"The pain's gone. It's a miracle."

"Who was that man?" Elliot looked at his mother. But it was Megan who knew the answer.

ELLIOT COULD NOT STOP talking about the incident. By the time they reached Megan's house, the headache she had originally invented to explain her quietness had become real.

She waited until Elliot had pulled out of the driveway, and his car was out of sight before she walked to her own car and started the engine. She pulled smoothly out of the driveway, not even veering an inch when Gino appeared beside her and said,

"Rather interesting afternoon. I haven't had that much fun since the chorus girls' convention in Vegas."

Megan checked right and left before pulling out into the street.

"The tango I learned from Bobby Duvall, but I thought the phantom mask was a nice touch."

Megan stared straight ahead, concentrating on the road.

"Not talking to me, I see. You're mad, aren't you?"

Megan didn't look at him, didn't speak to him.

"Well, could you, at least, tell me where we're going?"

Megan finally turned and looked at him. "To find the crock pot."

Chapter Six

Neither driver nor rider spoke for three miles. Gino reached into his pants pocket and pulled out a wadded paper.

"What do you know? The old gal slipped me her phone number."

Megan glanced at the wrinkled napkin on his lap. She saw it was blank. Her lips wanted to smile. She forced them into a sigh. "What exactly did you think you were doing back there? Did that little show have a point or do you just have an uncontrollable need for exhibition?"

"An out-of-control exhibitionist? *Moi?*"

"I'm serious, Gino."

"Was it that bad?"

"You pranced into Elliot's mother's house in thong underwear and tangoed like some sort of demented Latin lover."

"That broad can take a pretty deep dip." He was actually smiling. "Who'd ever thunk it?"

She stepped down on the accelerator.

"Do you always drive too fast?" he asked.

"Not until I met you," she answered between clamped teeth.

"I'm a bad influence?"

She sighed again. "I don't know what you are. But I do know I can't have you flaunting your, your…" She stuttered for a suitable word. "Charms all over Connecticut."

He received her scolding with a smug smile. "I get it. You're jealous."

"I'm what?" The speedometer needle jumped.

"There's no reason," he appeased. "I did it all for your benefit."

"My benefit?"

"Did you expect me to just hang out and watch that woman humiliate you? Elliot was no help."

"Leave Elliot out of this, okay? And Dolores wasn't humiliating me."

"No. Then what do you call that little tête-à-tête I witnessed?"

Megan eased up on the gas. Her shoulders slumped, all the fight leaving her body. *"Interacting?"*

"Maybe that's what Elliot would call it."

Megan stared at the road before them.

Gino's voice lost its teasing tone. "I wanted that woman to leave you alone. I was trying to get her mind on something else."

The unexpected sound of Megan's laughter filled the car. "You did that."

Chuckling, she turned the car left and pulled in behind the Crelco plant. "And it was nice of you to heal her hands," she noted.

"I told her." Gino leaned toward Megan and said in a half whisper:

"Be kind to all you meet. Or your hands will come back crippled. And so will your feet."

Megan hit the brakes too hard, throwing Gino backward. "You cursed Dolores?"

He gave her a cagey grin. "Some would call it a blessing."

"You can't do that."

He looked at her straight-on. "Yes, I can."

She didn't know whether she should hit him or hug him. She lifted her arm. Her slender wrist swiveled, showing another hand he'd made ivory-smooth. "Did you curse or bless me?"

Gino came close once more and caught her hand half-turned. "What do you think?"

Even if she knew the answer, she couldn't say it. She couldn't speak, she couldn't think—not with Gino so close, the strong lines of his face lifted with laughter. She watched the laughter level off, leaving behind a smile and a sweet wash of breath touching her face.

She looked away from the caress in his eyes, uncertain if it was real or only her own unspoken wish.

Their hands stayed bound. Her heart was beating hard, fast, the blood surging through her limbs. The stillness in the car became a held breath. She knew she had to look at him. She had to find the answer.

She met his gaze. Was the same wonder in her own eyes? Did he see her wish for him to kiss her? Did he see every cell of her body begging her to say her desire out loud? And once said, it would be impossible not to say it again. Her remaining wishes would be spent. Gino would be gone. She'd have nothing.

Except two kisses. A moment of complete happiness.

And the memory of a man like no other.

She lowered her head. She didn't need to look for the answer anymore. There was only one truth, and she already knew it as she had always known it. In the end, it made no difference if Gino cared for her. In the end, he'd go.

"What's the verdict, Megs? Cursed or blessed?"

She pulled back at the sound of his voice, her spine hitting the door handle. She lifted her head, her lips parting in a stiff smile. "I guess I'll have to stop being kind to you and find out."

"Kind to me?" Gino snorted. "You haven't even thanked me yet for this afternoon."

"Thanked you?" She returned his snort. "For what? Bursting into my future mother-in-law's living room and doing a bad imitation of an AWOL Chippendale dancer?"

"You'll thank me." Gino nodded knowingly. "When you and Elliot and Dolores become one big happy family in that two-bedroom, one-bath bungalow."

"I'm not living with Dolores."

"No? Where's she going to be? Elliot hasn't built the gazebo yet."

Megan looked front. "I'm not living with Dolores."

"That's not what Elliot said," Gino said pointedly.

Megan stared out the windshield. "I can't believe he never even discussed it with me. Never even mentioned it," she said more to herself than Gino.

"I can't believe it, either," he agreed, properly indignant.

Megan turned her head to him as if remembering he was there. "Like I said before, this isn't about Elliot. It's about you and your fancy footwork. And handiwork."

She tried to withdraw her own hand from his grasp, but Gino held it firmly. He stared down at it. His finger traced the back of it where the bones stretched long and elegant.

"My mother had lovely hands. Everyone said she was the most beautiful human ever to come to Heaven's Lower Regions. Like an angel fallen from above. But she left, and I've never been able to remember her face. All I remember are her hands." He turned Megan's hand over, his finger now touching where the skin was like down.

"Where'd she go?" Megan asked.

He shrugged. "Humans don't last long in my world. Their powers are too primitive."

"Your father was King. Why didn't he protect her?"

"They'd already mated," Gino said as if that explained everything.

"He wouldn't marry her? Not even after he found out she was pregnant?"

"Genies don't marry. They mate."

Megan let out a low whistle. "Talk about every male's fantasy come true. This father of yours, the King, who is he really? Hugh Hefner?"

Gino chuckled. Megan didn't.

"My mother was only one of my father's many mates."

"She had his son."

"A son only two-thirds genie."

"So?"

"You forget, only a full-blooded genie can rule the Upper Tier. His only heir, a half-breed, born of a mortal's loins. My father would not have anything to do with me."

She knew Gino would never allow the pain to show, but Megan didn't have to see it. She felt it, as swift and sure as her own soul turning inside out.

"Who took care of you?" she asked softly.

"The Fairies of the South until I came of age. Then, as a warrior, my exploits were unequaled throughout the Realms. Still, to the King, I might've been no more than the weak Women of the Mist."

"Because you're one-third human?" Megan tried to understand. "No offense to your father, but it does take two to fandango."

"Elliot's mother would drink to that."

Megan might have laughed if she wasn't so angry at fathers who could abandon their own children.

Gino's grip on her hand loosened. "Once I fulfill the curse, the Goddess will erase my flawed heritage. I'll become a full-blooded genie and be seated on the throne taken from me by a seductress's secrets."

Megan couldn't believe a minute ago she was empathizing with this chauvinistic snake charmer. It was easy to expand her anger from fathers she'd never know to a closer target.

"Well, right now, we need to find the crock pot taken from you by a master's mistake." Snatching her hand back, she reached for the door handle.

"You're angry again? Women!" Exasperation cracked his voice. "The final frontier!"

"That's right, Mr. Hocus-Pocus," Megan said to him. "You and your kind don't know beans about women."

Gino smiled a too easy smile. "I've lived two thousand years on your earth. I've traveled the width and depth of many dimensions, some which'll never be seen by human eyes. So, I feel safe in saying I speak for all of the male species when I say…" He leaned in close. "Who does?"

Megan swung the door open hard, its hinges crying out. "It's a good thing you genies don't have any powers when it comes to love. You'd really mess things up."

"No, you do that well enough on your own."

She stopped, half out of the car. "What's that supposed to mean?"

"Do you love Elliot?"

"Exactly what does that have to do with anything?"

"I don't think you do," Gino said matter-of-factly.

"Suddenly you're Cupid?"

"No, I've met Cupid. The man's a control freak."

Another time she would have laughed. "You're trying to distract me from finding the crock pot." She swung her other leg out of the car. "It's not going to work."

As she was about to stand up an overhead door in the warehouse opened. A tanker truck, the Crelco logo emblazoned on its side, pulled out.

"That's weird." Half crouched, she watched the tanker cross the field behind the plant. "They took away our Sunday shifts last November."

The truck disappeared into a stand of trees at the edge of the open space. "Maybe some cleanup needed to be done while the presses were down," she thought out loud. "Elliot would've worked, though. He never says no to double-time."

Gino looked at her hiding behind the door. "Is there a problem?"

"I didn't expect anyone to be here until third shift tonight," she explained.

Gino looked toward the far end of the field. "So we could garbage pick in peace?"

"Believe me, it's not my idea of a fun Sunday."

"We could go back to Elliot's mother's house," he suggested. "I bet the roast is ruined by now, though."

Megan slid back into the car seat and shut the door. "We'll have to wait for these guys to finish."

The tanker reappeared between the pines and started back toward the plant.

"I don't think they saw us," Megan said. "That

pile of skids there should've blocked their view. As soon as they're inside, I'll back the car up.''

The tanker made two more trips back and forth, the second time followed by a garbage truck.

''What're they doing?'' Gino asked.

''Crelco must dump its garbage back there,'' Megan answered.

''Isn't that illegal?''

''Not if it's safe waste. What does Elliot call it?'' She thought for a few seconds. '''Environmentally sound.' It's hazardous waste that causes all the problems. Elliot talks all the time about the thousands of dollars it costs Crelco each month to get rid of its toxic trash.''

''Sounds like fascinating pillow talk.''

Megan attributed the heat crawling up her cheeks more to anger than embarrassment. She sent Gino a sharp look. ''I'm beginning to understand why that Goddess cursed you.'' She turned her attention back to the tanker heading toward the trees.

''Is that where our crock pot went?'' Gino asked.

''Probably. Just pray it isn't buried by now.''

After the truck's last trip, two men came out and walked around a material silo. From behind the metal tower, a red-and-black pickup pulled out and drove away.

Gino looked at Megan. ''Looks like the coast is clear.''

They waited ten minutes, then Megan started the car and headed toward the trees. ''Actually it's a good thing I saw the men dumping or I would've never known about this place. Elliot never mentioned it.''

Past the trees, the path sloped down, stopping at a large pit far below filled with garbage. Megan eased the car down the steep, sandy trail and parked. Before they even opened the doors, a stinging odor filled the car.

"I thought you said they didn't dump hazardous waste back here?'' Gino said.

"They don't.''

"Then what is that smell?''

"ACK. Acethyl ketene. It's used as a sealant on filter bowls.''

When they stepped outside, the smell was so sharp, Megan took an unconscious step backward.

Gino blinked, his eyes beginning to water. "This stuff is safe?''

"When I was an operator, I worked with it almost every day.'' Hoping Gino didn't notice her holding her breath, she started to walk toward the garbage. The ground was soft beneath her feet.

He followed a few steps behind her. "They're allowed to dump this stuff right on the soil like this?''

"Of course.'' Megan continued toward the trash. "All Crelco's dangerous waste is shipped out. Elliot told me. The federal government doesn't fool around with companies who deliberately contaminate. They've sent company personnel who've authorized illegal dumping to jail. Elliot talks about it all the time.''

She was forced to inhale through her nose. The air

burned the delicate tissue inside her nostrils. "ACK is as safe as mother's milk. It's just in mass quantity, it gets a little nasty. A pit full of Limburger cheese would probably have the same effect." She took a big step forward.

"What was that?" Gino asked, halting Megan's intrepid progress.

"What?" She came back to his side, all brave pretense gone.

"Didn't you hear it?" They were both still. "It was like a rustling."

They stood motionless until the scurrying sound was heard again. Megan moved closer to Gino. "Rats?"

"I hate rats. And if they've been feeding off of this stuff, they're probably two-headed and glow green." Gino stepped back. "I'm not going any farther."

"Wait a minute." Megan put her hands on her hips. "Aren't you the same guy that used to slay dragons and punch out giants?"

"That was two thousand years ago. I've matured."

"You're really afraid of rats?"

"I'm not afraid to admit it. I'm a nineties man, at least, for the moment."

The scratching movement began again. Gino backed up until he was against the car's hood.

"You're serious?" Megan couldn't hide her grin. "Don't worry. I'll protect you. Come on out, you two-headed, slime-spitting rat and fight like a...a...a vermin."

A piece of wood shook. From behind it, Megan saw two round, brown eyes ringed with white.

"How do you feel about raccoons?" she yelled to Gino.

"Is it rabid?"

"It's not frothing at the mouth. And it only has one head."

The raccoon blinked twice, then turned and scampered away from the dump.

Gino came closer to Megan. "Raccoons I can deal with. But rats..." He shivered. "They give me the creeps."

Megan chuckled as she started back toward the trash. "You're only human."

"Just one-third," Gino said, correcting her.

She turned an assessing gaze on him. "Close enough," she decided.

For two hours, they carefully picked their way through the garbage not already buried by dirt.

"Are you sure it's here?" Gino asked.

"No, I'm not sure," Megan snapped.

"Hey," he stated. "I'm not the one who threw out my current quarters."

"Sorry." She rubbed her forehead. "I've a tremendous headache." She reached into her pants pocket and pulled out a tissue and blew her nose. When she lowered the tissue, she saw it was full of blood. "Oh, my goodness."

Gino looked her way. "That's it. We're out of this toxic-waste site." He took her by the arm before she could protest.

"I'm just not used to ACK because I haven't been exposed to it as much since I started working in Quality Control," she argued.

Gino kept a firm grip on her upper arm as he moved her toward the car. "Exposure time is over for today."

"But the crock pot?" she protested.

"We'll figure something out." He opened the driver's door and motioned for her to get inside. "Unless there's an army-navy surplus store open somewhere that'll sell us some gas masks," he said as he got into the other side. "This landfill is off-limits."

Before she could even put the key into the ignition, Gino started the car and steered it up the embankment.

"Okay, okay," she relented as they reached the top of the pit. "At least, let me drive."

"Just stay under the speed limit," he warned.

Megan drove slowly home, her thoughts concentrated on her current situation. They didn't find the crock pot, which meant Gino would stay within five hundred feet of her at all times until she made her two wishes.

He wasn't that bad to have around, she rationalized. As long as he kept his clothes on and didn't change into plant matter.

He could make her laugh. She snuck a side glance at his striking profile. She checked her gaze back to the road, but her heartbeat stayed quick. He could make her feel like no one else ever had.

He was like no one else, she reminded herself. He

was more than a man. He was magic. And with him by her side, she had no choice but to believe in magic.

Yet, all the wizardry and the witchery in the world wouldn't change the fact that Gino would leave as suddenly as he came.

He would go. Forever.

"So, if you don't love Elliot, why are you marrying him?" Gino broke into her thoughts.

Megan turned the car onto her street. Mrs. Coons's fat tabby sat beneath a streetlight and watched them pass.

"I never said I didn't love Elliot."

"You never said you did," he countered.

"Maybe I'm like you." Megan saw that Billy McGee had left the bike he just got for his birthday in his front yard again. "I don't need love."

"Yes, you do," Gino insisted. "All humans do—especially the females."

Megan turned into her driveway and parked the car. "This female needs a man who'll be there at the end of the day. A man who'll be a good husband and a good father. That man is Elliot."

She got out of the car and walked toward the house, indicating the discussion was over.

Gino followed her into the house. "I knew you didn't love him."

In her heart, Megan knew the words Gino said were true. She became angry. "You know nothing about love," she reminded him.

"Obviously neither do you."

"I'm not discussing this any longer." She marched

out of the room. When she came back, she carried a plastic basket of dirty clothes.

"I've more important things to do," she told Gino.

He was behind her as she walked down the stairs to the basement.

"That's right," he mocked. "Laundry, shopping lists, taxes, working for the next thirty years in a place that'll slowly cripple your body and seize your soul."

Megan bent down and began to separate soiled socks from dusty T-shirts. Towels worn thin were detached from nubby sheets. "It's called life," she said calmly.

"It's closer to death."

Megan threw clothes into the washing machine. She said nothing.

"Even Elliot, the prince of practicality, admits that," Gino said pointedly.

Megan slammed the machine's lid and stared at a crack in the concrete wall. "Soon, even Elliot will know there's no pot of gold at the end of the rainbow, no fairy godmothers." She bent down as if she were an old woman and picked up the laundry basket. "No Prince Charmings, no Sleeping Beauties," she murmured.

Gino touched the rim of the empty basket she held. "There's me."

She said nothing. She had no defense.

"After granting your last two wishes," Gino said, "I'll return to my world and achieve the one dream even I never dared to desire. I'll become a full-blooded genie and ascend to the throne with honor."

His hand moved away from the basket to Megan's bare arm, but before he touched her, she stepped back.

"All is possible," he said. His hand remained in the air.

Megan brought the basket up higher against her chest. "It's easy for you. You breeze in here, all smoke and show, preaching the impossible. But two more wishes, and you'll be no more than a memory." She took a deep breath. "A memory so unreal, I'll never be quite sure I didn't dream you."

"I'm real, Megan." He stepped closer to her, his hand still outstretched.

She moved back. "No, you're not."

"Don't be afraid."

"I'm not afraid. I'm just realistic." She set down the basket atop the washing machine and rubbed her forehead. "All I wanted was a crock pot to make soup in, spaghetti sauce, a stew now and then. That was all I needed."

Gino's hand dropped to his side. "I'm sure Dolores will throw you a dilly of a bridal shower, and you can put crock pot first on your wish list."

His sharp tone drew her attention. He looked back at her, his gaze coming down the aquiline slant of his nose until it settled around her. He didn't have to say the thought trying to burst past the wry twist of his lips. It was expressed in the calm condescension of his stare:

Humans!

She leaned against the washing machine. It welcomed her with a slow, easy churn. "You know, you may be all-powerful, but if it wasn't for me, you'd still be lounging around Club crock pot.''

"Meaning?" It was a cool cross-exam.

"Meaning I'm the master." She thought she'd experience more satisfaction at the look that skimmed his regal countenance.

His composure returned quicker than it left. "Yes, you're right. I've no business interfering. I apologize."

His unexpected humbleness caught her off guard.

He took a long breath as if weary. "It's only because when I'm high on my throne, I'll remember you. And I'll smile." He smiled then, but there was a soft spray of sadness in his eyes. "I'll be happy. I only want you to be happy, too."

He began to whirl, spinning like a dervish. "Call me, Master, when you want me."

"No—"

He spun faster into a funnel cloud.

"Wait—" She reached out a hand to stop him, but he was a reeling blur. The crack in the concrete suddenly split, and he was gone.

She stared at the wall, the crack again no more than a hairline. She reached over and touched the concrete, as solid as stone beneath her fingers.

"You son of a...a...a genie king." But even as she swore, a smile started and became full.

She may be the master, but he was the magic.

Chapter Seven

"So, is Gino still here?" Kitty asked.

Megan's head shot up, her half unwrapped sandwich forgotten. She looked at Kitty, Elliot, then back to Kitty.

"Gino?" Elliot lifted his own sandwich and took a bite. "Who's Gino?" he said, a dab of mayonnaise on his lower lip.

"Megan's pen pal," Kitty explained. "You haven't met him?"

Elliot looked at Megan. His chews became longer, slower. "No."

Oh boy, Megan thought. When she'd walked into the break room this morning and seen the crock pot still sitting on the counter, she'd thought her problems were over. She'd run with the pot to her car where Gino was stretched out in the back seat, munching a cherry cheese Danish and reading the sports section.

"Ta-da!" She'd presented the crock pot. "It was right on the break room counter where I'd left it. Elliot must've forgotten to put it in the garbage bin."

Gino had smiled wanly. "Bully for Elliot. And to

The Harlequin Reader Service® — Here's how it works:

Accepting your 2 free books and mystery gift places you under no obligation to buy anything. You may keep the books and gift and return the shipping statement marked "cancel." If you do not cancel, about a month later we'll send you 4 additional novels and bill you just $3.34 each in the U.S., or $3.71 in Canada, plus 25¢ delivery per book and applicable taxes if any.* That's the complete price and — compared to the cover price of $3.99 in the U.S. and $4.50 in Canada — it's quite a bargain! You may cancel at any time, but if you choose to continue, every month we'll send you 4 more books, which you may either purchase at the discount price or return to us and cancel your subscription.

*Terms and prices subject to change without notice. Sales tax applicable in N.Y. Canadian residents will be charged applicable provincial taxes and GST.

If offer card is missing write to: Harlequin Reader Service, 3010 Walden Ave., P.O. Box 1867, Buffalo NY 14240-1867

NO POSTAGE
NECESSARY
IF MAILED
IN THE
UNITED STATES

BUSINESS REPLY MAIL
FIRST-CLASS MAIL   PERMIT NO. 717   BUFFALO, NY

POSTAGE WILL BE PAID BY ADDRESSEE

HARLEQUIN READER SERVICE
3010 WALDEN AVE
PO BOX 1867
BUFFALO NY 14240-9952

Play The Lucky Hearts Game

and get... FREE BOOKS, a FREE GIFT... and MUCH more!

Yes! I have scratched off the silver card. Please send me my **2 FREE BOOKS** and **FREE MYSTERY GIFT**. I understand that I am under no obligation to purchase any books as explained on the back of this card.

Scratch Here!
then look below to see what your cards get you...

354 HDL CNFU

154 HDL CNFT

Name

(PLEASE PRINT)

Address   Apt.#

City   State/Prov.   Zip/Postal Code

Twenty-one gets you
2 FREE BOOKS and a
FREE MYSTERY GIFT!

Twenty gets you
2 FREE BOOKS!

Nineteen gets you
1 FREE BOOK!

TRY AGAIN!

Offer limited to one per household and not valid to current Harlequin American Romance® subscribers. All orders subject to approval.

PRINTED IN U.S.A.

think, we risked chemical contamination trying to find it.''

''I told you ACK only smells bad. Otherwise, it's harmless or they wouldn't be dumping it out back. Listen, I've got twenty minutes before my shift starts, so—'' she'd lifted the cover off the crock pot ''—jump in, and I'll run you home.''

Even now, she could see Gino's expression. Without a protest, without one word, he'd done as she'd asked. He didn't have to say anything. The angry look on his face had said it all.

''I suppose it wouldn't really matter if you waited until we got home to go undercover,'' she'd said to the crock pot.

When there was no response, she'd peered inside, but didn't see anything. She'd waited a few minutes, then replaced the top and started the car.

''It's for the best,'' she'd said as she pulled out of the parking lot, the crock pot on the seat beside her. ''Especially after your floor show at Elliot's mother's house yesterday. What if Elliot saw you and realized you were the fan dancer from his mother's living room? It's for the best, really,'' she'd repeated.

Not very skilled at making small talk with an appliance, she'd fallen silent, driving with one hand on the steering wheel, the other steadying the crock pot. She didn't speak again until she put the crock pot on her kitchen counter.

''I think you'll like this spot,'' she'd said to the cooker's clear cover. ''The sun hits here most of the afternoon.'' She'd laid her hand on the cover. ''Have a nice day, Gino.'' Her hand had rested on the glass top a minute more, then she'd left.

"SO, IS HE STILL VISITING you?'' Kitty asked.

Elliot looked at her, waiting for her answer.

Oh boy, Megan thought once more. ''Yes,'' she answered. She saw Elliot's thin eyebrows rise. ''And no.''

Elliot's brows angled with puzzlement.

''He arrived on Saturday, but he's been in and out since then.''

Elliot's brows pulled into a straight line, indicating displeasure. ''You didn't mention you had a houseguest?''

''He came so suddenly, dropped right out of the blue. That's crazy Gino.'' Megan laughed. Elliot didn't. ''I've no idea how long he's staying, and he's been so busy.''

''Doing what?'' Elliot asked evenly.

She smiled weakly. Several seconds passed. Finally she was inspired. ''Looking for living quarters.''

''He's moving here?'' Kitty asked.

''No!'' Megan attempted to temper her loud denial with a smile.

''Then why's he looking for a home?'' Kitty persisted.

''Not exactly a home.''

''Property?''

''Yes.'' Megan nodded as if she liked the sound of that. ''Property.''

''He buys and sells real estate?'' Kitty inquired.

Megan considered the idea. "I know he's owned two thousand properties during his...career."

"Wow!" her friend said.

"Megan." Although Elliot's voice was a normal speaking tone, it sounded louder as if the strain of remaining silent for the last few minutes was taking its toll. "Who is this person?"

She toyed with the plastic wrap on her sandwich. "He's a friend." She patted Elliot's hand. "That's all. I'm sure you've had friends I've never heard about." She paused before adding, "Like Kimberly."

EIGHT MILES AWAY, Gino had his own problems. Besides feeling nauseous from the stench of stale corned beef and cabbage, he still couldn't sleep. His genie side could probably continue this way for many more days, but his human side required rest soon. It had been over two days since his last shut-eye and, at this point, he was ready to give up his promised kingdom for ten minutes of deep slumber.

Last night, after he'd left Megan in the laundry room, he'd become air, certain the ethereal form would free him from human thoughts, emotions. Desire. No more than lightness itself, he'd risen, seeking the peace and relief of dreamless sleep.

He'd needed space. He'd needed distance to try to understand what was happening to him, why he was becoming so personally involved in a master's life. It shouldn't matter to him that Elliot's mother had mistreated Megan. It shouldn't matter to him that Megan was going to marry Elliot and make a big mistake. None of this should matter to him.

But it did. It mattered more to him than he wanted to think about. So, he'd floated up, rising into the sky five hundred feet above his master, hoping the thoughts could not follow a vapor, the feelings could not find near nothingness.

But one memory had filled the void. Fly as high as he could, he remained haunted, possessed by the picture when Megan had come to him, and they'd danced together on a nearly deserted island. He'd held her in his arms and, for the first time in his life, he hadn't felt two-thirds genie, one-third human, a foot in both worlds, never completely belonging in either. He'd felt whole. He'd thought such joy would only be attained when sitting high on the royal throne, surveying his kingdom.

He'd never imagined it was a feeling he'd find on earth in the arms of a mere human.

Soon the sky had become cloaked with clouds, and he'd become rain, falling softly back to the earth where Megan walked.

ELLIOT WAS SILENT AGAIN for a frozen moment until he summoned her name once more. "Megan."

His voice was now lower. Megan recognized the tone. When Elliot got mad, he didn't yell or swear. No, he didn't rant or rave. He became "reasonable."

"I'd like to meet your friend." Elliot interlaced his fingers. His hands were set on the table in a cool curve. "Would that be possible?"

"Well…" What if Elliot recognized Gino as the G-stringed gigolo who bumped and grinded in his mother's living room yesterday, then performed a minor miracle before disappearing into thin air? How would she explain that?

"Are you saying I can't meet your friend? I don't understand." Elliot's hands knotted together.

"Of course, you can meet Gino," she assured him.

Elliot waited. "When?" he finally asked in that ever-patient tone.

"When?" Megan echoed. "*We-e-e-l-l-l,* like I said, I never know when he's going to pop in. He's in and out all the time."

Elliot's hands, still bound in a fist, tapped the tabletop. "Maybe you could try calling him?" he suggested logically.

"A barbecue!" Kitty exclaimed.

Megan and Elliot looked at her as if she'd lost her mind.

"Tonight's my Lovely Lady Lingerie party, remember, Megan?" Kitty went on. "And Elliot, you're coming over for Monday night poker with the men. So, why don't you both come over a little early, bring Gino with you, I'll put a couple of T-bones on the Miracle Thaw, we'll drink a few beers and all have a real good time."

Kitty sat back in her chair, crossed her arms beneath her ample chest and smiled, satisfied she'd found the answer to all their problems.

Elliot looked at Megan. "Sounds good to me."

"Me, too," she agreed lamely.

"Do you think Gino can make it?" Kitty asked.

"I don't see any reason why he couldn't," Elliot stated, aiming a pointed look at Megan.

She couldn't think of a reason either, at that moment, but she'd make sure she had a good one by the time she showed up at Kitty's tonight—*sans* Gino.

"We've got to get back to work, don't we?" She attempted to end the conversation.

Kitty glanced at the clock. "Goodness, you're right." She started to gather her lunch wrappings. She took a final sip of her coffee as she stood up. "I've got to stop at the ladies' room quick. Elliot, I'll see you tonight around five-thirty. Megan, I'll see you down in Q.C."

As Kitty left, Megan started to rewrap her own uneaten sandwich. She gave Elliot a quick glance. He was watching her, a paragon of calm. Her fingers fumbled with the plastic wrap, which refused to cooperate. Finally, with a sigh, she got up and threw the sandwich and the balled-up plastic wrap into the trash can. Elliot watched her walk back to the table.

"Something wrong?" he asked.

She didn't sit down. She crumpled her napkin and brown lunch bag. "No, no. I've got to get back to work." She picked up her unopened can of diet cola, ready to go.

"Megan." Elliot stopped her. "Is there something you'd like to tell me?"

Even she heard the nervous denial in her light laughter. "No, of course not."

Elliot sat there, his hands still folded, a sensible

sphinx. "I'm looking forward to meeting your friend, but I'm still not clear why you didn't mention him to me before. If Kitty hadn't brought him up, I wonder if you would've told me about him at all. He must've been there the night I brought you home from the accident."

Megan sat down. "Elliot, Gino isn't a person. I mean he isn't a people."

"What?"

She took a deep breath and attempted to dig herself out of the hole she'd just made deeper. "What I'm trying to say is he's not a people person. The truth is he doesn't think much of the human race as a whole. Sometimes, he finds his own private space and doesn't see anyone for long periods of time."

"He sounds a little strange."

"He's different."

"How long have you known this guy?"

"Not very long."

"Are you sure he's safe to have in the house?"

"Believe me, he wouldn't hurt a fly. And once you get to know him, he's not that strange. In many ways, he's like you and me."

Elliot's hands flattened on the tabletop. "Why didn't you tell me about him?"

She had a sudden inspiration. "I did."

Elliot gave her a level look.

"Remember on Saturday, when I left that message on your machine, telling you to come over to the house quick? That's when Gino first arrived, and I wanted you to meet him. At that time, he expected to be here for only about an hour. I didn't mention him again, because I thought he'd gone, but that's not how it worked out. He'll be around longer than he expected, so now, there's time for you to meet him." She stood up. "I've got to get back to work."

Elliot looked at her. "As I remember, on that message, you also told me to bring my .38."

"No, I said…don't be late." She tried to leave.

"Megan?" Elliot's summons stopped her once more. "Kimberly and I had planned to marry, but while I was away in the marines, she started seeing other guys."

"You don't have to talk about it," Megan said softly.

"No, I want you to know. I didn't find out it was all over with Kimberly until I got back home. She said she was sorry. She loved me but she couldn't marry someone like me." Elliot looked away, staring at the selections on the soda machine.

"Someone like you?" Megan asked, not understanding.

Elliot shrugged. "Middle class, blue collar, uneducated. She was beautiful and brainy. She was going to be a doctor. She felt she could do better. We've seen each other a handful of times since then. She's been divorced twice."

"It seems she found out what we already know," Megan said.

Elliot's gaze came back from a far-off memory. "What's that?"

"She can't do better than you."

Elliot smiled. "If she doesn't know it by now, she will shortly."

Megan's smile grew puzzled. "What do you mean?"

"One day soon, Kimberly is going to be surprised," Elliot said.

"You're talking crazy again." Just like yesterday at his mother's when he'd rambled on about gazebos and bidets.

He winked at her as he stood up to go, that tight, small smile still on his face. "Crazy as a fox."

THE Q.C. OFFICE was still empty when Megan returned from lunch. She went into the back testing room to finish the measuring she'd started before lunch. She was adjusting the gauges when Kitty appeared in the doorway.

Kitty raised a white bucket. "I got the one o'clock shots."

"Good. I'll help you measure them as soon as I finish impact testing these flanges."

Kitty set down the bucket. "Megan, I'd no idea Elliot didn't know about Gino. I never would've brought him up if I'd known. I'm sorry."

"You don't have to apologize. I talked to Elliot after you left, and we straightened it all out. Everything's fine."

"You're not mad?"

Megan patted her friend's forearm. "There's nothing to be mad about."

Relieved, Kitty plopped down onto a stool inside

the doorway. "I'm looking forward to tonight. It'll be fun, and I've got to admit, I'm a little curious about this mystery man myself. Is he single, because I've got a cousin who's—"

"About tonight," Megan interrupted.

Kitty looked at her and waited.

"I don't think it's going to be possible."

Kitty's features puckered. "Why?"

Megan rubbed her forehead. Here we go again, she thought, having to come up with a logical explanation for a completely illogical situation. But it would only get worse if Gino went with her to Kitty's tonight. Kitty herself had just expressed her curiosity, and Megan knew Elliot would give Gino the third degree. All those questions with no acceptable answers. That was the main reason Gino was staying home tonight. That and the fact she never knew what he might do, say or conjure.

"You are mad, aren't you?" Kitty's pink-frosted lips began to tremble.

"No," she insisted. "It's not that at all."

Tears welled in the other woman's eyes.

"Don't cry, Kitty. I'm not mad." Megan pulled up another stool and put her arm around her friend's shoulders. "Really, I'm not."

Kitty sniffed loudly. "Don't mind me. I always get like this right before my time of the month."

Megan hugged her friend a little harder. Kitty and her husband, Mark, had been trying to have children for the last eleven years of their twelve-year marriage. Megan rummaged in her jeans' pockets and found a couple of crumpled but clean napkins. She handed one to Kitty. "Are you sure?"

"I've got all the symptoms. Bloating, tiredness. I've had a headache for two days, and last night, I bawled over one of those AT&T call-home commercials." Kitty blew her nose loudly.

"You'd think," she said, "after all this time, I'd get used to it. But I never do. Each month, I chart my temperature, nag Mark about wearing boxer shorts, stand on my head after sex. Each time, I'm sure will be the moment we'll create a miracle. Then, each month, I begin to bleed."

Megan rubbed her friend's back.

"Mark's done the doctor visits, the tiny room with the plastic specimen cups and the old issues of *Playboy.* I've had my pipes cleaned out and taken enough fertility pills to populate a small, underdeveloped country."

Megan handed her friend another wrinkled napkin.

"The adoption agency has such a long waiting list, they're not even taking any more applications right now. We don't have the money for a private adoption. We used up all our savings on the medical tests and specialists' visits."

Kitty's tears fell faster. "As a teenager, my biggest fear was I'd get pregnant. Now, as an adult, my biggest fear is I won't."

Megan put her arms around the other woman and drew her to her chest. She felt the bony line of her friend's spine as it rippled with each soundless cry.

She rocked Kitty side to side as if the woman were a child herself.

In the outer office, a door opened, and they heard the sounds of voices.

Kitty lifted her head. "Arnold must be back from lunch."

Megan took the wet tissues from Kitty's hand and gently wiped her mascara-streaked cheeks.

"I must be a sight. Hormones," Kitty said disgustedly. "Listen, don't worry about tonight. I understand."

Megan took Kitty's hand. "No, you don't."

Kitty looked at her.

And I can't explain it to you, Megan thought, looking into those black-ringed raccoon eyes.

"We'll be there," she said.

The smile she saw on Kitty's face made her doubt all her fears. Maybe it won't be so bad, she reasoned as she followed Kitty into the outer room. *We'll eat a little steak, I'll buy a negligee I'll never wear, Elliot and Gino will lose at a few hands of poker. Just a normal night out for a girl, her boyfriend...*

And her genie.

GINO WAS STILL WIDE-AWAKE when he heard the back door open. He heard Megan say his name.

He stood up and began to pace, following the never-ending curve of the crock pot's walls, the thoughts that had plagued him all afternoon making his steps quicker.

She was the master, and he was the servant. She

was a human; he was a genie, soon to become king of his own kind. Her life was here. His life was about to begin in the Upper Tier.

He heard her say his name again, the sound of her voice sweeter than the angels' hymns heralding a new day.

For two thousand years, he'd been halfway between heaven and earth, exiled from his own world, never completely belonging to hers. Then, two wishes away from his long-awaited desire, he'd met a deeper desire, a more powerful need. He could almost hear Ishtar's laughter above.

He sat down, folding his arms across his chest. He'd battled beasts with the strength of wild animals and the cunning of gods. He'd mocked creatures with the blackness of evil in their eyes. He'd spurned the Goddess of Love and War. He'd have no problem resisting a human woman.

She said his name once more as she lifted the cover off the crock pot and peered in. She couldn't see him, but he could see her, so close, yet always a world away from him.

For the first time in two thousand years, he felt cursed.

"We have to talk about something," Megan said into the seemingly empty crock pot. She waited a moment, then said, "It involves lingerie."

"Frederick's or Victoria's?"

Megan spun around. Gino was sitting at the kitchen table, nonchalantly peeling an apple. Megan didn't know which was more disconcerting: his abrupt disappearances or the sudden return of his face and figure, his very beauty belying his human form. He smiled at her. It was truly unfair for a man to be so handsome that every time she looked at him, reason scattered and desire reigned.

"We're going out tonight," she said.

"Really?" The peel came off the apple in a clean, complete piece. "Just where does the lingerie come in?"

"Remember my friend, Kitty? You met her at the plant Saturday."

"I remember." Gino sliced his apple in half.

"She's having a lingerie party tonight and—"

"If you volunteered me to model the G-strings—"

"No, I didn't volunteer you to model the G-strings." She started to laugh, realizing it was the first time she'd laughed all day. "Why? Did you want to?"

"Not especially." He cut his apple once more.

"I thought you enjoyed that line of work."

"Even us crock pot dwellers have a little dignity."

She realized how much she'd missed him today. She'd missed the way he could make her laugh and even the way he could make her crazy. She'd missed the way he could make her feel like nobody else ever had. Or ever would. The thought came so quickly, she barely had time to suppress it.

"Here's the story. Kitty's invited us and that means you and me and Elliot—"

"We're a ménage à trois now?"

"To her house for dinner around five-thirty. Afterward, some other couples are coming over. The guys are going to play poker during the girls' home lingerie show.''

"Life in the fast lane, huh?''

''Just don't drink too many Bud Lights and start telling your life story.''

Gino made a face. "Killjoy.''

''Listen, we're going to have enough trouble explaining you. If you start that Prince of the Gin Rummy shtick, they're going to be sending the men in the white jackets for you…and me.''

''Don't worry. I've been doing this for two thousand years. I know the routine.''

''You'll be good?''

''I'll be great.''

Megan smiled but worry still pleated her brow as she started toward the hall. "I'm going to go take a shower.'' She stopped at the doorway. "You're not going to do your rumba routine tonight, are you?''

Gino stood up to throw away the apple peels. "Not unless Elliot's mother requests it.''

"Elliot's mother at a lingerie party? Hardly.''

"You never know.'' He put his knife in the sink and rinsed his hands. "After yesterday, she may be a changed woman.''

''You'd better hope she isn't there, or you and I are in deep doo-doo. I'm worried enough Elliot'll recognize you, but he only saw you for a split second, and your face was half covered. Besides, this time, you'll have your clothes on. Right?'' Megan emphasized.

Gino gave her a long, level look ending with a slow-motion blink. "How's this?" he asked.

He wore baggy plaid boxer shorts, a Hawaiian print shirt unbuttoned to reveal a T-shirt underneath sporting the Tasmanian Devil. On his head was a baseball cap that said Hair Today...Gone Tomorrow.

"Get serious, please. Tonight's going to be difficult enough. Now blink on something beige." Megan almost made it to the hall this time before she stopped.

"You're not going to cheat at cards, are you? I mean, with your special talents, you could wipe these guys out, and Elliot's been acting really strange when it comes to money lately. You'd think he had an endless supply stashed away. I know he may have a little savings, but that's it. You heard him talking to his mother about the big house he wants to buy. I don't know why he goes on like that. The reality is we both may not even have jobs in another few months if the talk around the plant is true."

"Maybe he has a genie, too?" Gino suggested.

"There's more of you around here?" Megan asked in alarm.

Gino looked away from her, down into the wild eyes of the cartoon character across his chest. When he looked up, his own eyes revealed nothing. "If you're so worried about me going tonight, why'd you say I'd come? I've my home sweet home." He indicated the slow cooker. "We're no longer joined at the hip, give or take five hundred feet."

Megan leaned against the doorjamb. "I tried to get

out of it. Believe me, I tried, but then Kitty got upset and started crying.''

''Because you declined her dinner invitation?'' Gino said skeptically.

''Sort of, no, not exactly. She was really more upset because…well, Kitty and her husband have been trying to have a baby forever, but it doesn't look like it's going to happen anytime soon.''

''I want to be clear on this—I'm going to a lingerie-poker party tonight because the hostess can't have a baby?''

''I know, it sounds ridiculous, but you should've seen her. I didn't have the heart to hurt her more. I feel so bad for her. She wants a child more than anything in the world. It seems like such a simple thing, but when something goes wrong, you realize it's really a miracle. And believe me, that's what Kitty needs…''

Openmouthed, Megan stared at Gino. A smile started across her parted lips.

''A miracle. Kitty needs a miracle.'' Megan's face filled with joy as she looked at Gino.

''And we could give it to her.''

Chapter Eight

"You could do it, couldn't you?" Megan's words tumbled out in one breath.

Gino lifted an eyebrow. "You've just taken the term 'social intercourse' to a whole new level."

"But it could be done?" she persisted.

"When would you prefer? Over guacamole and chips or when we're sipping internationally flavored coffees after dinner?"

"You could do it," she decided. She laughed. "I mean, you don't actually have to do it." She stopped laughing. "Do you?"

"Procreation without the pleasure? I thought that went out with the fifties?"

"Can you do it?" Megan's voice was half plea, half prayer. Her hands rose in appeal.

He took her hands in his. "Make a wish."

She looked up into his eyes, and a calmness and certainty came. "I wish..." Her tone was hushed and reverent. "For Kitty Sue Wasniewski to be with child."

Gino's eyes closed. He lifted her hand to his lips

and kissed the valley between her knuckles. His eyes slowly opened.

"It is done."

They stood very still as the wonder of life wrapped around them.

"You've a wonderful gift." Megan's voice was still hushed.

"At the risk of bringing up bad memories, I must remind you it takes two to fandango."

Megan's smile was softer than Gino's voice, softer than her palm pressed against his. She looked down at their hands still clasped together.

She could have let go then. He could have released her.

Their fingers tangled together neither tightened nor relaxed. She was so close, he could see the fine down on her cheeks, a stray hair beneath the plucked line of her eyebrow. She lifted her head, and in her eyes, he saw desire.

His head bowed in homage, drawn to the naked need in her eyes, knowing too sharply the same want within him. His lips parted, he breathed, but still he was choking. His mouth began to move blindly, seeking salvation from the flesh of her shoulder, her throat, her own lips gasping for air. He covered her mouth with his, giving her the last strangled breath burning his chest. She took the gift he offered and gave it back to him multiplied. Feeling, deep and dizzying, flooded his body as if life had just begun.

He drank, a starving man now gorging himself. Her lips equally hungry, opened wider, allowing him to taste and touch and marvel at the very miracle of woman. His hands left hers to wrap around her waist. He held her tight as if she would slip away as suddenly as a dream. She folded against him, as warm and soft and sweet as a summer's shower. All went still except their hearts.

It wasn't until she pulled away from him, her head twisting in a wrenching movement, that his reason returned. She stepped back, her chest rising and falling, her breaths coming too fast. He reached out for her, to stay her. She turned her head to him, her eyes bright, her lips thick from his kisses. She gave him her hand.

What was he doing? He was a prince one wish away from his throne. She was a mortal woman engaged to marry another. He had no right to touch her, to need her, to want her so, to want her still.

Should he say he was sorry? Certainly what he'd done was wrong. Yet it felt nothing but right—more right, more perfect than he'd ever expected to know. How could he betray something so beautiful, so rare with an apology? How could he temper the feelings raging inside him with a false expression of regret?

She smiled then, absolving him completely.

"I've got to get ready to go to Kitty's" was all she said. She let go of his hand and left the room, all the emotions and questions left unsaid.

MEGAN CLOSED HER BEDROOM door and sat down on the edge of the bed. She folded her hands in her lap and was motionless, her spine straight. She sat suspended, very still, barely breathing, like one not wanting to awaken from a dream.

She should feel guilt, remorse, shock.

She knew only joy.

Soon enough the other emotions would come to pummel her conscience. They would plague her, reminding her she was engaged to one man, but kissing another—another who was not a man at all, who, at times, seemed no more than a figment of her imagination.

Yet it wasn't her imagination that had kissed her only moments ago. It had been a man—living, breathing, flesh and blood. It had been a man who had taken her into his arms and spoke to her in the secret language of desire. And it had been a woman who had answered him. In the kitchen, when they had come together in passion and need, there had been only a man, only a woman.

She chased out the accusations already gathering strength. Regret would come all too quickly later.

Now was her moment—hers and Gino's. In those brief seconds, convention had fallen away; propriety had been passed over. Two hearts had met and whispered joy. One touch of his lips, and the impossible seemed possible. People could disappear into nothingness. They could be swept backward in time. They could fall in love. She knew all these things now, and the knowledge had come in one kiss. Right or wrong, she could not be less than grateful.

She sat a minute longer, then exhaled and stood, rising to get ready to meet the man she was to marry.

THEY DROVE TO KITTY'S house, their thoughts each of the other, the taste of Gino still fresh and full on Megan's mouth. The air in the car was too close. She opened the window. The scent of the freshly cut grass swept inside, its smell cloyingly sweet.

She braked left into a development of short streets and abrupt corners. The houses were all the same, varying only in color and the number of ceramic gnomes on the front lawns. She pulled into a stone driveway leading to a low-peaked ranch, its vinyl siding the color of the faded denim shorts worn by their approaching hostess. A ceramic frog beside the front door held a small sign that said Welcome To Our Pad.

She turned off the engine. Gino reached for the door handle.

"Is there anything else we should've done?" she had to ask.

He considered her question. "A shrimp ring would've been a nice gesture."

She laid an anxious hand on his forearm. "Is Kitty really pregnant?"

He placed a reassuring hand on top of hers. "Probably with twins. I do have supernatural powers, you know."

She laughed. He looked down at their hands, his broad square covering her narrower width so he couldn't tell where one hand ended and the other began.

He looked up. Her laughter had settled into a smile. The small space in the car seemed to contract further. He remembered the moist heat of her mouth, the unspoken need of her body pressed to his. She sat still. He made no motion. Yet, they seemed to be moving toward each other, drawn like two polar ends. He made himself look away from her gaze. The first time could be forgiven; the second time would be deliberate.

She slid her hand out from beneath his and opened the car door. He stepped out also, meeting Kitty's scarlet-lipped smile.

"Gino, I'm so glad you could make it. Come on out back. Mark's on the patio watching, oh, I'm not sure. One of those baseball teams with a bird name— Orioles, Blue Jays, Woodpeckers.

"You like baseball, Gino?" Kitty continued, heading toward the back.

Megan stopped midstep, praying Gino wouldn't answer his preferred sport was streaking across the desert, robes streaming, scimitar risen, the smell of slain monsters' blood filling the dry night air.

"Doesn't every self-respecting American male love baseball?" he replied.

Kitty laughed. "But not every self-respecting American male's wife."

Megan allowed herself a smile. Maybe this evening wouldn't be so bad after all.

They rounded a corner to the backyard. On the deck, a large, solidly built man was reclining in a lawn chair, a remote control resting on his chest.

"This is my husband, Mark," Kitty introduced.

Mark got up from the lounge chair. Its webbed seat retained his shape. He set down a beer can and wiped his wide hand across his batik print shorts before extending it to Gino.

"Good to meet you, buddy. Take a load off." He indicated the matching recliner next to his. Both were angled toward the portable television in the corner.

"Kitty says you're here on business?"

"My work brought me here, yes," Gino confirmed.

"Well, I'm glad you have time for a little pleasure, too."

Gino accepted the beer Kitty offered him and popped open its top. He raised the can in a toast. "To pleasure."

"I'll drink to that." Mark took a long sip from his own can. He glanced at the muted television screen in the corner.

"How long have you known Megan?" he asked, his gaze shifting away from the silent screen.

"We've known each other…" Gino looked at the television. "Hey, that hit looks like it's going all the way."

Mark grabbed the remote and turned up the volume. The announcer's voice blared out "…say goodbye to that one, ladies and gentlemen. It's every player and fan's dream—a grand slam in the bottom of the ninth."

"All right." Mark grabbed his beer and took another long swallow. "We'll get these guys to the World Series yet."

Kitty looked at Megan and rolled her eyes. "These boys have all they need—baseball and beer. C'mon inside. I want you to try this new dip recipe I made.''

Kitty started toward the back door, not noticing Megan's hesitation. Megan looked at Gino stretched out in the lounge chair, his beer can balanced on his belly. He glanced up at her.

''It wasn't even a pinch hitter,'' Mark was saying. ''It's that bum with the lowest RBI in the league. He hasn't had a home run all season. If I hadn't seen it with my own eyes, I wouldn't have believed it.''

Gino winked at Megan and smiled. She sent him a stern look signaling ''that's enough.''

''Megan,'' Kitty called through the back door screen.

She started reluctantly toward the house, giving Gino one last look of warning over her shoulder.

Kitty was in the kitchen opening a bag of potato chips. ''I'm really glad you came,'' she said.

Megan stayed at the back door, looking out to the deck.

''Is everything all right out there?'' Kitty asked. ''You don't think Gino feels out of place, being the new kid on the block and all?''

''Oh, no.'' Megan turned from the door and walked over to the kitchen table. ''Don't worry about Gino. He's very adaptable.''

Kitty placed the bowl of chips on the table. ''And don't worry about me. I won't start sobbing into my Jell-O salad during dinner.''

''Everything's okay.'' Megan said it as a statement, but Kitty interpreted it as a question.

"Let's just say I'm not the basket case I was this afternoon," she answered as she opened the refrigerator and took out a pitcher of lemonade. She poured a tall glass for Megan. "I'm sorry."

Kitty reached behind her for the glass of wine on the counter. "Sometimes, this whole thing gets the better of me." She took a sip.

"Do you thing you should be doing that?" Megan blurted.

Kitty looked at her strangely. "I don't see any good reason why not." She waved the glass of wine in the air. "Cheers."

Megan watched in alarm as her friend took another drink. She had to stop her, not only for her own health but for the health of her baby. But how? She couldn't just tell her the truth.

She took a big breath. "Alcohol has been proven harmful to unborn fetuses."

Kitty looked at her over the rim of her glass. Her eyes filled with heartbreaking confusion and pain.

"How could you say…?" Her voice cracked. She put down the wine.

"Listen." Megan set down her own glass of lemonade. "You say you feel tired, moody, fat—"

"I'm aware of how I feel." Kitty cut her off.

"They could be the symptoms of PMS."

Kitty folded her arms beneath her chest. Her jaw was so tight, it trembled.

"They could also be the symptoms of pregnancy," Megan added softly.

Kitty's jawline went slack. "You, of all people, know how painful this is for me."

"Have you gotten your period yet?" Megan pressed on.

"No, but—"

"So, how do you know you're not pregnant?"

"I know," Kitty insisted.

"How?"

"I don't feel pregnant."

"Have you ever been pregnant?" Megan countered.

"You know the answer to that."

"Then, how do you know what it feels like to be pregnant?"

Kitty was silent.

"C'mon, let's go get one of those home pregnancy tests. They're supposed to be accurate." Megan headed toward the door. She looked back at Kitty who hadn't moved.

"If it's negative..." Kitty's voice trailed off.

Megan walked back to her friend and put an arm around her shoulders. "What if it's positive?"

"It'd be a miracle."

"Miracles can happen," Megan gently insisted.

"Well, I haven't seen one lately. Have you?"

Yes, Megan thought, and, for a moment, she was back in Gino's arms again. She looked into her friend's eyes and smiled reassuringly. "Then, the odds are in our favor." She squeezed Kitty's shoulders. "Let's go get that pregnancy test."

Kitty's expression was both hopeful and scared.

"I've got three in the top drawer of my bedroom dresser."

"You've been holding out on me all this time?" Megan turned her friend around and steered her toward the bedroom.

Kitty's hands trembled as she held the first test strip. So great was her fear and hope, that she began to cry while waiting for the results. When it showed positive, her tears fell harder and faster, her knees buckled, her breath began to come in short gasps. Megan was crying almost as hard before the second test was finished. By the time the third test came out positive, the two women were crying and choking on their joy.

"It's as if you knew," Kitty sputtered. Her face was translucent, a masterpiece of happiness.

Megan took her friend's hand. "I only wished for it with all my heart."

"Hey." Mark's voice came from the doorway. He took in the tearstained faces of his wife and her best friend. "Is everything all right?"

Kitty, just beginning to retain control, started to cry all over again. Mark rushed to her side, his features tightening with worry. "Honey, what's wrong?"

Kitty wrapped her arms around her husband. "Nothing. Absolutely nothing."

Before Megan reached the kitchen, she heard Mark's wild whoop. Smiling, she crossed the kitchen. Again she heard another gleeful shriek. Only it didn't come from the bedroom behind her. It had come from the backyard. Megan stopped smiling.

She hurried to the door, stopping short before the screen, her eyes widening. On the deck, Dolores was moving across the grass green carpet toward Gino.

"It's him. It's him," she rejoiced before seizing Gino around the middle and wrapping him in a tight embrace. Elliot watched, looking as if he was sucking on something sour. His gaze lifted, and he saw Megan standing at the screen door.

She came out and stood on the deck. "I guess introductions aren't necessary."

With a pretense of embarrassment, Gino gently disentangled himself from Dolores's arms. He looked above her to Elliot's stoic stare. Gino shrugged sheepishly. "I'm often mistaken for Fabio."

Dolores laughed, waving away his comment with a graceful sweep of her healed hands. The rings she wore on almost every finger caught the light of the sun. Her nails were lacquered a brilliant red.

"Do you know what I did today?" she confided to Gino. She raised her other hand and displayed it with a delicate twist of her wrist. "I had a manicure."

"Your hands are lovely," Gino assured her.

"Thanks to you," Dolores gushed. She took his hands in her new ones. "Thank you for dancing into my life yesterday." She beamed up at him until emotion overcame her once more, demanding another hug.

"Megan." It was a summons. "I'd like to speak to you." Without waiting for her answer, Elliot walked toward the front of the house. Megan glanced at Gino helpless in Dolores's embrace, then started after Elliot, feeling equally helpless.

Elliot walked to the end of the driveway, then turned on his heel. Gravel skittered across the grass. He said nothing, his lips colorless. The breeze had stopped. Fury hung so heavy in the still air, Megan waited for it to curve the boughs of a sapling on the corner.

She didn't know what to say, but she had to say something. "Dolores is going through her change, isn't she?"

Elliot wet his lips with the tip of his tongue. "Explain to me again who this Gino is."

Megan took a step backward, away from the aura of his anger. "He's a friend."

Elliot nodded as if he understood. Megan knew he didn't. "Tell me." He took a step toward her, bringing her back into the circle of his contempt. "Is he also a friend of my mother's?"

Megan fought to stay even with his stare. "She seems to think so."

"So, they've met?" he cross-examined.

"What do you mean by 'met'?" She evaded his question.

"What I mean is—" his voice rose to the roar of a wounded animal "—why is my mother back there hugging some stranger who likes to sleep at my fiancée's?"

He turned away from her. She saw his shoulders jerk once. She lightly touched his back and felt him stiffen.

"My girlfriend forgets to mention that a mystery man has moved in with her. A man does a bump and grind, then disappears, during Sunday dinner at my mother's. That night my mother starts to sing 'Great Balls of Fire.'" He turned slowly and looked Megan squarely in the eye. "My mother doesn't sing."

"Perhaps she never had a reason to before," Megan offered.

"Well, she has a reason now." Elliot puffed a breath of disgust. "She's happy. You know my mother, she's never happy."

Megan had to smile. "But, Elliot, being happy is good."

"Some stranger sashays across my mother's shag carpet and, all of a sudden, she's doing a Jerry Lee Lewis lounge act. That's not good. That's bizarre."

Megan laughed out loud. "I think it's good to see your mother smile."

"And my mother doesn't hug," Elliot went on. "But right now, she's in a choke hold with Little Italy back there. How do you explain that?"

Megan half smiled. "Hospitality?"

"Did you hear what she yelled? 'It's him!' As if the Second Coming had started. You don't find all this unusual, or am I the only sane person here?"

Megan's grin vanished. "Did the doctor increase your mother's estrogen supplements?"

"She thinks the man in her house yesterday and the man back there are one and the same. So do I."

Megan's stomach tightened. She chewed the inside of her cheek.

Elliot tipped his head to one side. Megan shifted beneath his study.

"My mother was made a fool of yesterday. Is it my turn today?"

"Let's go back and join the others." Megan attempted to change the subject.

He ignored her suggestion. "You've been different, too, for the last few days," he remarked.

"Kitty made a new dip. Let's go try it."

"You're jumpy, nervous, distracted—ever since your friend came."

Megan took several steps backward. "I really think we should get back to the others."

Elliot refused to let her leave, "That's what he is, isn't he—a friend?"

"Yes, that's what he is—a friend."

Elliot kept her centered in his sight. "Nothing less...nothing more?"

"I'm going back." Megan started to walk away.

"Are you sleeping with him?"

She stopped. Her head pulled back as if she'd been slapped. Instantly she remembered the kiss, the taste, the touch of Gino. So vivid was the memory, his hands could have been on her now, smoothing the curve of her spine. She turned and faced Elliot, and if the guilt was not on her face, it was in her heart.

"How can you even ask such a thing?" was her automatic denial.

Elliot inhaled deeply as if struggling for control. "How can I not?" He crossed the space between them and grasped her arm. "Who is he, Megan?"

She looked up into his face. A muscle quivered across the length of his throat. She could feel his vulnerability as if she'd reached up and touched that trembling flesh.

She had never meant to hurt him, and she told him now.

His grip tightened on her forearm. "So, it's true?"

"No!" Her protest was loud and immediate.

He looked down at her, his eyes staying dark with doubt. He opened his mouth but didn't speak. He dropped her arm and began to pace in a small circle.

She made a move toward him, but stopped. The emotional distance between them was much greater than any physical closeness could gap. She watched him circle, wondering what she could say to him, what could she tell him to take away his anger, to bring back his trust?

There was only one answer: the truth.

Even the idea of it made her inhale sharply and hope for a sudden storm, a bolt of lightning, a wind so strong shingles would fly from the roofs, anything to avoid this moment. Elliot endlessly circled. Megan's thoughts went round and round.

She'd hurt him. She'd broken his trust. She'd lied; she'd evaded. She was no better than the men who had wooed her mother, and then wandered off. She was no better than those she'd despised. Elliot deserved better.

He deserved the truth.

But what if he didn't believe her?

He was the man she was going to marry. If he

didn't believe her, who would? She was to be his wife, and if everyone else said she was crazy, he'd say she was sane. If everyone else called her story a lie, he'd state it as fact. If everyone else laughed and pointed, he'd stand by her side.

"Elliot." She reached out her hand, but he didn't take it. "Come with me. I want to show you something."

Chapter Nine

When Megan reached the backyard, she saw that Kitty and Mark had come out to the deck. Mark was lighting the grill. Kitty was sitting at the picnic table, smiling ecstatically. Dolores was there, too, her smile approaching Kitty's rapture. Gino sat in between the two women, an expression on his face as though he'd eaten too many green apples.

"Okay," Megan instructed Elliot. "Have a seat."

"Megan," he resisted. "Exactly what's going on?"

She smiled reassuringly. "Just have a seat, and you'll see."

She stood in front of Gino and the others. "Dolores, you're right. Gino was the one who came to your house yesterday."

Dolores clapped her new hands together. "I knew it." She smiled at Gino.

Gino looked at Megan with interest.

"As far as I know, the dancing was an impromptu performance. He has much greater gifts than that."

"Amen," Dolores said.

"For example." Megan looked at Elliot's mother. "He cured Dolores's hands." She looked at her friend. "And he made Kitty pregnant."

There was a large crash as the platter of steaks fell. Mark came toward the picnic table, a long-handled spatula raised menacingly, his chest rising and falling beneath a chef's apron that said Best Beef In The East. "He's mine."

Elliot sprang up. "I want a piece of him first."

Gino stood up and snapped his fingers. Both men froze midstep, their faces contorted with anger. Kitty and Dolores were also as still as statues. Megan waved her hand in front of Kitty's eyes. Nothing. Not even a blink.

She looked up at Gino. "What'd you do?"

"Let's not worry about what I'm doing," he said. "The question is what are you doing?"

"Elliot thinks we're sleeping together. I have to show him you're a genie."

Gino rubbed his chin, then glanced back at Elliot poised with one hand curled into a fist. "You'd be safer with the imagined infidelity."

"What?" Megan was indignant. "I should let Elliot think we're having an affair when nothing could be further from the truth. Yes, there was that one kiss, but that meant nothing, absolutely nothing." She gave Gino a sidelong glance.

"Of course, it meant nothing," he too readily agreed.

"Two comrades merely celebrating a successful conclusion."

"It's not every day you create a child," he observed.

"It was a kiss for good luck," she offered.

"Just a way to say 'job well done.'"

"I'm an engaged woman, after all."

"I'm the future king of my kind."

They eyed each other. Megan was the first to speak again. "So, there's absolutely no reason for Elliot to suspect anything. My only choice is to prove you're a genie."

Gino looked at Elliot, then back at her. "Are you sure?"

She nodded.

"You're taking a big chance."

"I have to," she said, resolved. "I don't want Elliot to leave me."

"You're the master." Gino snapped his fingers once more. The others came back to life.

Mark lunged toward him. "You low-down—"

"Mark!" Kitty vaulted between her husband and Gino. Mark stopped short. Elliot, one step behind him, crashed into his backside.

"I've never been with this man." Kitty gestured toward Gino.

"No, of course not." Megan came up beside her. "Kitty having an affair with Gino is as ridiculous as…as me having an affair with him or…or Dolores here."

"Now, hold on," Dolores protested. "I may be old, but I'm not dead." She smiled at Gino.

"What I'm trying to say is…is…" Megan held out

her hands as if trying to pluck the right words from thin air. She glanced at Gino who watched her with amused detachment. "Oh boy, I guess the only way to say this is to come right out and say it…Gino is a genie."

Silence followed her statement. Megan saw a look pass between Kitty and Mark.

Dolores said, "I thought you told me you don't drink."

"I don't," Megan insisted. "And I'm not crazy. Listen." She told Gino's story beginning with the curse and ending with the second wish. "I know it sounds unbelievable, but it's the truth." She looked point-blank into Elliot's eyes. "I swear."

There was more uncomfortable silence until Mark began to laugh. "Good one, Megs. I gotta admit you really had us going for a minute there."

Kitty looked uneasily at Mark, making a shushing motion with her hand. "I think she really believes it, honey." She sent Megan a worried look.

"You got him at a yard sale, you say?" Dolores questioned. She gave Gino a once-over. "And I thought I got good buys at Wal-Mart."

"Elliot?" A note of plea strained Megan's voice. "Do you believe me?"

Elliot was staring at Gino. "No, I don't believe you," he said, the anger controlled and cutting in his voice. "I don't believe you'd go to these lengths to humiliate me."

He started to turn away.

"Elliot, wait," Megan begged. "Watch," she

asked as his steps stopped. "Okay, Gino, do that disappearing thing you do."

Gino, his face impassive, blinked once and was gone.

"See." Megan turned to the others, triumphant.

Elliot snorted in disgust. "What's he going to do next? Pull a rabbit out of his hat?"

Megan's shoulders sagged. "Okay, Gino, c'mon back."

Gino reappeared, his face still expressionless. Kitty gave a little gasp.

"Big deal," Elliot said. "David Copperfield made the Statue of Liberty disappear. And even he doesn't claim to live in a brass lamp."

"Megan said he lived in a crock pot," Dolores said pointedly.

"What about your mother's hands?" Megan submitted.

She felt a glimmer of hope as Elliot studied his mother's hands.

"She started new medication about a month ago. The doctor said that, combined with the uncommonly hot, dry weather we've been having this summer, probably eased the stiffness and pain."

"What about Kitty's pregnancy?"

"You and your genie did that? And I always thought the stork brought the babies."

"What do I have to do to convince you?" Frustration and desperation mixed, turning Megan's voice raw.

"Let me see." Elliot considered her question. "You said you have one wish left?"

She nodded.

"Well, then," he said as if the answer was obvious. He looked directly at Megan. "Make it."

"Make it?" she repeated in a softer voice.

"What's the problem? You said he gave you three wishes. The first you used when you rescued Frank from an accident no one ever heard of, but, let's not split hairs. The second one you used to make Kitty pregnant. Did you know that, Mark? All that time you'd been trying when you could've been down at the Bowl-n-Brew, working on your seven-ten split. That leaves one wish left."

Elliot fixed Megan in his sight. "Make it."

She shifted her weight from one foot to the other. "It's not that easy."

"No?" He was incredulous. "What's the problem? The man's a genie, right? Right?" he insisted when Megan didn't respond.

"Yes, but—"

"He can do anything you ask him?"

"Not everything."

"No?" Elliot said with more mock amazement.

"He can't give me more wishes."

"Fair enough."

"He can't make someone love me."

"Is that what you wished?" Elliot demanded.

"No," Megan hastily replied.

"Any other restrictions?" Elliot asked with a barely sufferable air.

She shook her head.

"Then, this man, excuse me, this genie hardly seems unreasonable. Go ahead, make your third wish."

She looked into Elliot's eyes. The irises were as colorless as one of the stones on Dolores's fingers.

"I can't," she said.

"No?" His lips went tight, sharpening the short lines around his mouth.

She looked down at the ground. "I don't know what I want." She looked back up at Elliot, hoping for understanding.

"It's evident you don't know what you want," he snapped back at her. "You should've told me that when I asked you to marry me instead of saying yes and then, making a total fool of me. That's what I wish. Unfortunately I don't have a genie to make it come true. C'mon, Mom, show's over."

"Elliot, no!" Megan cried.

He wouldn't even look at her. "C'mon, Mom."

Dolores reluctantly got to her feet. She looked wistfully at Gino. "You weren't going to dance at the lingerie party, were you?"

Elliot disappeared around the corner.

"Oh, I better go be with him. Kitty, I'm sorry," Dolores apologized before hurrying after her son.

Megan sank down into a lawn chair as if the simple act of standing required too much effort.

"Perhaps, we should go, too," Gino said. He stood behind her and placed a gentle hand on her shoulder.

She allowed herself to be led to the car. He opened

the passenger door for her. He buckled the seat belt snug across her body.

"I should've had you do something else," she was saying as he slid in behind the wheel. "That thing you do with the trees and the gems. Now that would've gotten Elliot's attention."

"It wouldn't have helped." He inserted the key into the ignition and started the car.

"Why not?"

He backed the car out of the driveway. "People believe when they're ready to believe. That's what I was trying to warn you about back there." He winked at Megan. "I think Dolores might be on your side, though."

"That'd be a first," she muttered. She stared out the window. Gino put the car into Drive and started toward home.

"What're you saying? It takes some people longer to believe than others?" she asked.

"Sure, some people take longer. Some people never believe—people like Elliot."

She turned away from the window. "Never? Why?"

"Some people can only trust what makes sense. I'm so completely outside the realm of their belief, I threaten everything they know as true."

"You do turn a person's world upside down."

"It didn't stop you from believing in me. In fact, you were one of the easy ones."

"Strange. I would've thought I'd be more like Elliot," she mused.

He glanced at her. "Maybe you're not as much like Elliot as you think."

"What's that supposed to mean?"

Gino's gaze went back to the road. "Maybe deep down, you were ready to believe, ready to trust someone."

"I had Elliot."

"Elliot's not here now." Gino looked at her.

"Your fiancée tells you she has a genie in her crock pot, and you don't expect the man to get upset?" Megan argued.

"Obviously you didn't," Gino said with maddening rationality. "Or you would've never told him."

"I thought he'd, at least, give me the benefit of the doubt," she conceded.

"If he loved you, he would've trusted you. And if you trusted him, you would've been able to love him."

He was right, but it only made Megan angrier. "Since when did you become Miss Lonelyhearts? They don't even have love where you come from."

"You hang around humans for two thousand years, you pick up a thing or two."

Megan stared unseeingly out the windshield. "I never expected Elliot to love me. I only expected him not to leave me."

She heard Gino's cluck of disapproval. "You ask the impossible."

She turned toward him. "What do you mean?"

"No one can give you that kind of security. Not Elliot. Not even me."

They'd come home. Gino waited until he'd parked the car and turned off the engine so he could look her right in the eyes. "Sometimes, the people that love you have to leave you. They might not want to, but, sometimes, they have no choice."

"Elliot had a choice," Megan maintained, although she had the feeling Gino wasn't talking about Elliot anymore.

"So did you."

She gave an indignant laugh. "What choice did I have?"

"You could've made the third wish."

Megan said nothing. There was no defense, no denial.

"Then Elliot might not've left you," Gino added.

But you would have. The thought rose immediately, not allowing Megan time to reject it. So strong, so swift was the truth, she turned away, afraid he would see the pain in her eyes. One last wish, and he'd be gone forever.

She knew the truth then. She could let Elliot leave her. She could suffer her friends' worried, curious looks. What she couldn't willingly bring about was Gino's goodbye.

She finally turned to him, not wanting to arouse his suspicion. "As you well know, I don't know what I want," she insisted in a clear voice.

He looked at her a moment too long as if he also knew the truth. How easy it would be if he laughed right now, scorning the certainty of her statement, calling her bluff.

Yet, what difference would it make if his contempt drove her to confession? What would it matter if she revealed she knew exactly what she wanted.

Her avowal of the truth would only lead to a greater truth: the one thing she wanted was the one and only thing she could never have.

Gino reached for the door handle without a word. Relief made her legs weak as she followed him inside the house.

"I think I'll hit the sack," she said as soon as they were inside. "It's been another long, strange day."

"You're not going to eat?"

"I'm not hungry. But you help yourself. There's some salad and soybean dressing in the refrig."

Gino made a face. "That's okay. I'll just whip something up." Platters of steak, baked potatoes and steaming corn on the cob appeared on the table. A basket of rolls nestled between the plates. Silver bowls of sour cream and butter completed the meal.

"Are you sure you won't join me?" he invited. "It's really no problem."

Megan mustered a smile, but shook her head. She started toward the bedroom, hesitating at the entrance to the hall. "What're you going to do after this?"

Gino looked up at her, puzzled. "I'm going to be King."

"No, no." She laughed. "I meant what're you going to do tonight, after you finish dinner?"

He leaned back in his chair. "Oh, I don't know. What time is it in Paris? If Marie-Anne Cantin's cheese shop in the Rue du Champ-de-Mars is still open, I could do with a bit of Brie and fruit for my dessert. Shall we take a chance?''

Frowning, Megan rocked back and forth on her heels. ''Couldn't you just blink it up?''

When he laughed, she realized he'd been teasing her.

''Don't worry,'' he assured her. ''After dinner, I'll curl up in my crock pot like a good genie.'' He turned his attention back to the meal.

At the doorway, Megan said, ''We humans must be such a dull lot to you.''

Gino was busy smearing sour cream across his potato. ''You have your moments.''

She smiled. ''I suppose. Good night, Gino.''

''Good night.''

Still she lingered in the doorway. ''If you'd be more comfortable, you're welcome to use the guest bedroom.''

Gino looked up from the roll he was buttering. ''Maybe I will. Thank you.''

She gave an odd half-laugh that caused Gino to continue looking at her. ''It feels like I should be the one thanking you.''

He put down the knife and roll. ''Why?''

''I'm not sure.'' She gave that strange yelp of a laugh again. ''You're over two thousand years old, you live in a crock pot, you make miracles with a blink. Yet, talking to you, being with you, everything seems to make sense.''

She shook her head, finally starting down the hall. ''It's crazy.''

LATER, STRETCHED OUT on the narrow bed, Gino saw only Megan's face. He heard again and again the words she'd spoken: *It's crazy.*

And he agreed.

He shifted to the side, trying to curl his legs beneath him to fit the short mattress but only succeeded in loosening the sheet in irritating wrinkles beneath him.

He sat up, forgoing sleep, knowing it was more than the uncomfortable bed or the twisted bedclothes that disturbed his rest.

At Kitty's house today, Megan could have made the third wish, and it would have been over. The curse would have been fulfilled. He would have returned to his world and received his well-earned reward. Megan would have married Elliot and had what she craved: a home, a husband, a family. Everyone would have lived happily ever after.

Yet, this afternoon when Elliot had asked Megan to make the third wish, Gino had suddenly forgotten how to breathe, his heart seemed barely to beat. He'd waited for Megan's answer, knowing it was more than the third wish. It was the last wish, the wish to end all others. He should have been praying to the gods for her to make it.

Instead he'd asked the exact opposite from the spirits above.

And when his prayer was answered, he praised the heavens in silent joy.

Gino's head fell back onto the flat, damp pillow. His hands rose, palms up. Why?

Why?

As if in echo, he heard Megan scream.

He was in her room before the scream peaked. The moonlight coming in through the window shadowed her prone form. She twisted onto her stomach, whimpering now, and he realized she was still in the throes of a terrified sleep. He kneeled at her bedside, smoothing back the moist curls from her brow, gently easing her from the arms of the dream demons.

"Megan," he said softly, careful not to snatch her back too abruptly. The devils of sleep needed to be sneaked up on or they only increased their hold, giggling with glee.

"Megan," he whispered again, barely shaking her, his voice a low call.

She sat up suddenly, snapping the demons' direct hold. But, in the glaze of her stare, he saw that she remembered their horrors. He sat on the bed beside her, holding her shoulders. Startled, she turned to him, then collapsed, her breaths labored against his neck.

"The blood, the blood," she muttered. "It was so red against the white satin gown."

"Shh." He quieted her down, smoothing her wet curls, rocking her gently, seeing that the night demons had done their damage.

"Then she was gone. My mother was gone. I was alone in the car, her blood staining my bridal dress." The words spilled from her as vividly as the dream's surreal images.

She looked up, still trembling from the night's black touch, still saying words only spoken in the dark. "Everyone leaves, Gino. They don't even say goodbye. They just go."

The moonlight streaked across her features, bringing luminescent life to her pain. "Shh," he said, trying to shelter her profile of strangely painted sadness back to his shoulder.

She fought against his soothing strokes, lifting her head. "You'll leave, too."

It was not a question. They both had known the answer from the beginning.

"Please, when you leave me..." Her words caught as if she could say no more. "Say goodbye."

Emotion overwhelmed his voice. He stared at her. His heart, having only known joy from her, now learned pain.

"Promise," she pleaded from the depths of her soul stripped bare by the night.

"I promise."

She smiled then, and he kissed her on the cheek, intending only comfort. But her head turned and their mouths met. Her lips were warm and alive, seeking him until the night seemed to fade. Together as one, they defied the darkness, feasting on the wetness and texture of each other until the demons scattered and their heads moved in a soundless, rhythmic lullaby.

When the kiss ended, all grew still, the night gods placated. As if exhausted from a great battle, Megan rested against him. He rubbed her back, and this half man, half immortal who had walked with gods and waltzed with goddesses, couldn't imagine more fulfillment than the fragile, fine feel of Megan's spine against his palm.

Her head weighted heavy against his shoulder and her breathing slowed, becoming light and even.

Carefully he eased her down onto the pillow. Her body stretched out in welcome.

He sat there, afraid to leave her once more alone against the evilness of the night.

His hand touched her cheek, her brow now as smooth as a child's. "Sleep, dear Megan."

Still he sat on the bed, unwilling to leave her unprotected against the creatures of deep sleep. He took her hand and held it to let the dream devils know they were battling two now. Her hand, small and soft, curled against his like a newborn kitten, and he met the miracle of human touch.

He looked at the woman now in perfect sleep, and knew why, had always known why, he had prayed against the third wish that day.

"Oh, Megan," he said simply, his anguish mixed with amazement. He lifted the tiny, unmoving hand he held and, closing his eyes, laid it against his cheek. She was his curse.

And his salvation.

Chapter Ten

The alarm went off at five-thirty, waking both Megan, who was curled up in her bed, and Gino, who was stretched out in the upholstered chair in the corner. Their first look at each other was filled with surprise, then they smiled, not unhappy to wake and find the other one there.

"Good morning," Megan said, her cheek pressed into the softness of the pillow. Her arms were wrapped around another pillow as if she was holding herself from a fall.

"Good morning to you." She was tousled and sleepy-eyed. She'd never looked more beautiful. He was pleased to see the dream demons hadn't done any permanent damage. The thought of waking each day to that face came into his mind. He didn't chase it out immediately.

She released the pillow and stretched, her limbs extending beneath the covers, moving with a slow welcome to wakefulness. The thin sheet outlining her figure turned and arched with the movement of her body. Gino looked away, feeling ridiculous for envying a mere cotton cloth.

"I must thank you," he heard her say. He looked back to see that she had turned on her side to face him, the bed sheet twisted tight around her form.

"Thank you for staying. The nightmares..." Her eyes closed; her mouth clenched.

"The nightmares," she said again. Her eyes opened but the tender skin around her lips remained taut. "They don't come as often as they used to. It was probably from being overtired, the fight with Elliot."

"You could wish for him back." He hated himself for saying the words. He would have hated himself more if he hadn't.

He saw surprise in the sudden lift of her lashes. "You told me I couldn't wish for love."

"No, I can't give you love. I can bring Elliot back to you...if you wish. The first has nothing to do with the latter."

Megan flopped down onto the pillow. "I refuse to argue about wishes and my relationship with Elliot before my first cup of morning coffee."

An oversize mug, steam lazily rising from its surface, appeared on the nightstand. Megan propped herself up on one elbow and looked at him. He saw the centers of her eyes, wide and exposed, soften like the liqueur middles of fine chocolates.

"Don't ever leave me," she declared in a Blanche DuBois Southern slur. But as she reached for the cup, he saw the sharp press of her mouth return, and he knew her jest had unwittingly brought back the night before.

"It is well within my powers to bring Elliot back to you. If you wish," he told her once more, only hoping to bring her happiness.

"I don't know." She set down the cup of coffee and rolled onto her back, her eyes trained on the slow-moving paddles of the ceiling fan. "I know you're anxious for me to make the third wish—"

"That has nothing to do with this."

Her head swung toward him. "Since when?"

He stood and walked to the window. He had known for some time, maybe from the beginning. Now, he heard the truth pronounced deep down, in the human depths of him. He didn't want to leave her. Yet he could not stay.

He pressed his forehead against the glass. He had been cursed long before his fateful meeting with Ishtar in the Great Forest. From his father, he'd received magic, cunning, courage, strength. But from his mother, he'd been given a human heart with all its excess of emotion and unlimited vulnerabilities. A human heart that now belonged to Megan.

He stared out the window. His destiny was in a different direction. He was to become King. Or remain a slave. His life could never be with her. His life would never be complete without her. He was forever cursed.

He sat back down in the chair, its uneven legs wobbling side to side beneath his weight. "Of course, I want you to make the third wish." Her face showed no reaction. He kept his expressionless. "But because I feel responsible for what happened between you and Elliot yesterday—"

"What do you mean?" She sat up, the sheet falling, revealing her upper body. Her shoulders were smooth and bare except for two thin, lace straps holding the cotton gown of yellow rosebuds that she wore. A satin bud, curled tight on the gown's neckline, dipped into the shadows between her breasts with each quick breath she took.

"If I hadn't danced with Dolores, she never would've recognized me at Kitty's yesterday, and then, you would've never had to explain to Elliot and, well, you know the rest. None of that would've happened if I hadn't flamencoed my way through Dolores's front door. I'm sorry."

Megan's hand twisted the rose between her breasts. "You were only trying to help me," she reasoned. "Plus you took away Dolores's pain."

"Dolores will heal herself with her own kindness to others."

Megan looked down at her own hand. It had left the flower to lay flat near her heart.

"Is that what you were trying to do when you removed my scars, my scratches, my rough skin? Take away my pain?" The hand he'd made smooth reached for the coffee cup.

He looked at her, the mug raised to her lips, her eyes half closed, watching him as she let the steam play upon her face.

Yes, he'd been trying to take away her pain, but

he now knew he'd been trying to allay his own pain, too. He had hoped to lessen the pain of leaving her, the pain of never being able to give her what she really wanted: a home, a husband, a family. He could not give her any of it.

He said nothing. What could he tell her?

All he could give her was one last wish. If this last wish was his to ask rather than grant, he'd wish to know what would make Megan smile like this every morning? What would make her sleep without waking with screams?

"It is my wish to make you happy, Megan."

She continued to stare at him through heavy-lidded eyes as if she saw past his genie facade.

"If you wish, I could make last evening completely disappear."

Her lids lifted, and he saw interest light in her eyes.

"Elliot, Kitty, Dolores, Mark, no one would re-member what happened. No one would know except you and me—just like the accident at the factory. Your life would continue on the path you'd chosen."

Megan looked down into her coffee cup, staring at its surface as if the answer would rise like the steam from the liquid. Indecision puckered her brow and he, the Upper Tier's most infamous warrior, felt his first tremble of true fear. What if she agreed and wished for Elliot back? Yes, he had to say goodbye one day, but not today. He wasn't ready to leave her, would never be ready.

Yet, if it brought her happiness, he would go.

Megan's head stayed bent over the mug of coffee.

She sipped, then tilted her head up. The steam had warmed her skin. Her eyes closed. Her features were still, her face an inscrutable cameo. Her head dipped again.

He closed his own eyes, unwilling to watch any longer. Two thousand years he had waited for this moment. Who would ever believe, now, when it was so near, he was terrified it would actually come to pass?

He supported his brow in his hand, his only consolation the thought of giving her happiness. That was all that mattered now. The throne, the end of the curse, all else was secondary to granting Megan her happiness. If he was the source, the wellspring from where her joy rose, no matter what else happened, he'd be the luckiest genie—and man—who had ever existed.

"No," he heard her say.

He looked up. "What?" he asked, not trusting he hadn't imagined his own reprieve.

"There's no one to blame for Elliot and me breaking up, except Elliot and me. If it happened that easily, obviously, it would've happened sooner or later anyway. All you did was save us from the terrible mistake of getting married. Thank you."

Gino held up his hands. "Please stop thanking me. I'm a genie, not a saint."

"A genie with a heart," Megan told him.

He looked at her lovely face, and the heart she spoke so highly of broke in two.

He stood up. "You'd better get ready to go to work," he said, walking out the door.

He was right, but she stayed in bed. One more sip of coffee, one more slow stretch, feeling her muscles lengthen, contract. How long since she'd lain in bed, merely marveling at the sheer wonder of being alive? She set down the coffee cup and curled on her side. Her eyes fluttered closed, not to sleep, but to immerse herself further in the contentment covering her like the sheet spread across her body.

She had no right to feel this way. Yet, it had been so long, perhaps never. Would it be so awful if she wallowed in it a little longer?

Later, she'd worry about a being, one-third human, two-thirds magic, who lived in a crock pot and could make her heart beat harder than she dreamed physically possible.

She'd seen him heal a hand, create a child, disappear into a crack in the wall, with nothing more than a blink of an eye. But it was this burgeoning rhythm of her heart, a song she'd never even imagined, that convinced her his powers were beyond compare.

She wasn't sure when it had started. There had been the feeling the first moment she saw him, a fluttering like butterfly wings trying to break free of their cocoon. There had been the comfort of last night, to wake and find herself no longer alone. Then, to sleep once more with a restfulness so satisfying, she'd woken this morning, knowing the nightmares would never hold her so closely again.

This, however, was a leaping-with-joy feeling, and

a far cry from her usual satisfaction of seeing another day through, knowing she had a job, a roof over her head, friends, health. No, this feeling was wilder and completely without wanting. It was full of wonder and all things wished.

Megan didn't know exactly when it had begun.

All she knew, all she'd learned, was it would end.

One more wish and it would be over.

Her eyes opened, and she sat up. She walked to the window where Gino had stood only moments before. The promise of a perfect day greeted her, mocking the sudden heaviness in her heart.

They would have today, she consoled herself. Certainly tomorrow and maybe the tomorrow after that. Who knows how long until a third wish could be chosen?

Megan turned away from the window. She'd take it one day at a time, one minute at a time, one moment. That was all she had—hours, minutes, moments. It had to be enough. She could wish otherwise with all her heart; she could summon Gino's omnipotent powers; she could rail against the injustice. It wouldn't matter. In the end, Gino would have to go.

MEGAN LEFT FOR WORK, and for once, Gino didn't mind going into the crock pot. It was like a meat-scented monastery—ideal for thought. His thoughts were of Megan all day.

For two thousand years, he'd thought of nothing more than the day he'd leave Earth, the image always a balm. Today also, he thought of the day he'd say goodbye to the humans, goodbye to Megan. Being gored by the Bull of Heaven would have been less painful.

Yet, he couldn't stay with her. Even he, who made the impossible possible, knew he had no choice. Megan would make the third wish, and then, he'd be before Ishtar once more. If the goddess was satisfied, she'd keep her pledge. He'd become a full-blooded genie, rightful heir to the throne of his father.

Any attempt to deliberately thwart Ishtar, to purposely deny or even postpone the third wish, would only guarantee the goddess's wrath. Loss of his magical powers was a certainty. Then, if Ishtar was merciful, she'd banish him. If not, he, a warrior whose majesty, strength and deeds of courage, had never been eclipsed in the history of heroes, would be forced to wander his world the rest of his days in shame, an easy prey for his many enemies.

Whether he fulfilled the curse or not, he wouldn't be allowed to remain here—with Megan. And she couldn't come with him. Humans were fair game in the Upper Tier. Even if he could protect her, he knew that was not the path to her happiness.

Let the third wish be given. Let it bring Megan happiness. Then, he would go. Their worlds would separate, but he would go freely, knowing the tears were only in his soul—not hers.

And so, he came full circle again, back to the question that had plagued him since he stood at the kitchen window this morning, waving goodbye to Megan.

What will make her happy?

He thought back over the time he'd known her. She had scorned his offers of wealth, showing her true nobility of character. She had used her first two wishes to help others, illustrating her wide generosity of spirit. Beauty had been bestowed on her at birth, along with a quick wit and admirable intelligence. She had spoken of security, but, even if she could capture that capricious quantity, she would achieve only sleepy contentment. That could not compare to the happiness Gino wished for his master.

He could grant her continued health, but what good was a long life without rapture? He could give her the wisdom of the ages, but endless intelligence without ecstasy would deteriorate into dullness.

He thought long and hard about his two thousand years here among the humans. They were a crude breed, silly, sometimes, as the spirit imps that lived in the sky; other times, heroic as the finest warriors roaming the heavenly levels. He had fulfilled many dreams. Had he ever given the happiness he now so desperately demanded for his Megan?

He knew it was possible. He'd witnessed it here on earth. The humans, joyous beyond belief, their very being riding on the wings of bliss. He'd even known it himself, yesterday, today, whenever the mere thought of Megan was his.

How much easier it was to think of her instead of this riddle he couldn't answer. He saw her again for the first time when he'd appeared in the kitchen: one tiny hand wringing the other, her brows pulled low, forming two slants at the bridge of her nose.

He saw her laughing, her features backlit with joy and the song of her glee like the fairies' serenade. He felt her dancing in his arms to endless music older than he. He could hear the words she'd said.

And the answer came, but not with the clang and the clamor he'd expected. Nor did it pierce his soul like the lightning bolts the gods toss for sport across the sky. Instead it came gently in Megan's soft voice, in Megan's whispered words, washing over him like the waves they'd danced to that morning on their private island. Gino wasn't aware he was floating until his head hit the crock pot's cover.

She'd told him then, when he'd held her against his heart and felt hers beat in answer. She'd said, *I'm happy now.* He had heard the words, but he hadn't been listening. Now the answer, once realized, seemed to shout out, showing him it had been there from the beginning. Their first night together, she'd asked, *Why can't you grant love?*

He'd forgotten her question in her talk about security and husbands and fathers who stay more than six months.

Now he heard it. He saw the sudden sadness that had come into her features. Her question endlessly circled the walls imprisoning him.

He fell to the crock pot floor, burying his head in his hands, begging for a return to his former state of ignorance.

He slowly lifted his head to gaze at the blankness before him. There was no turning back. He now knew the one thing Megan wanted, the only thing she needed to bring her happiness.

And it was the one and only thing he could never give her.

MEGAN PULLED INTO the driveway a little after three that afternoon. She stopped the car and turned off the engine, but she didn't get out. She sat, holding on to the steering wheel, her gaze straight ahead. Gino walked toward her, wondering what she was looking at. When he got closer, he saw she wasn't really looking at anything, just staring off into space with the saddest expression he'd ever seen on anyone, human or immortal. Her pain mirrored the agony etched on his own heart. He knew too well the source of his sadness. What could cause Megan such great grief?

"Megan?" he said gently.

She looked up, startled, and he saw she hadn't known he was there. The sadness slipped smoothly off her face, her expression turning seamless.

"Would you like to go on a picnic?" she said. "I know the perfect spot."

The sunlight spilled into the car, gilding her features, entwining her hair with threads of gold. She gave no acknowledgment of his astonished expression.

"I'll pack some food and drinks." Her voice was light, but still he sensed her heart was troubled.

"Do you fish?" she asked as she got out of the car.

It was obvious she wasn't going to talk about what

was bothering her. He followed her into the house. "With a pole?"

"Of course. What else?" She looked at him as if remembering who she was talking to. "Never mind. Don't answer that."

She collected the things they needed in record time, as if they didn't have a minute to spare. They packed the car and climbed inside. Gino switched on the radio, and the car filled with music. He started to sing off-key. Megan smiled, then joined in on the chorus. To an outsider, they would have been just another handsome, young couple carried away by the call of the sun and the flawless blue sky and the ever-present nearness of each other.

"Gino?" The song ended. Megan sent him a quick look. "No magic, okay?"

"Okay."

But there was magic that afternoon. It was in the way the trees bent over a grassy square, allowing only a dappling of sunlight, just enough to warm Megan's bare arms. It was in the song of the katydids and lazy hum of the bees nearby, welcoming the man and woman. It was in the touch of Gino's fingers when he took her hand to help her down the rocky embankment to the flat ground below. She had forbidden any magic, but, as if in deliberate defiance, it was everywhere.

She spread the plaid throw across the grass and sat, feeling the coolness of the ground beneath her bare thighs. Gino set the ice chest on the edge of the blanket. Megan unclasped the barrette holding her hair back, and with a small twist of her neck, her hair spilled across her shoulders. She closed her eyes and tilted her head back to the warmth above, the raining sunlight coloring the inside of her eyelids.

She opened her eyes and saw Gino studying her. He didn't look away immediately.

"Are you hungry?" She opened the cooler and looked inside. "We've cheese and yogurt and ham." She started to spread food in a semicircle around her. "We've fruit, freshly baked bread. Even beer brewed with Rocky Mountain water," she read from the front of the can.

She laughed then for seemingly no reason at all. She popped open the top of the metal can, a small spray wetting her fingers. She kissed the moisture on her fingers while offering the beer to him with her other hand. The can was smooth and cool; his touch, when it met hers, searing.

She uncapped a bottle of fruit juice for herself, but did not drink. Her hands moved across the food, stopping and choosing a bunch of grapes, ham rolled tightly into a spiral, a generous square of soft yellow cheese. Gino slowly sliced the round loaf of bread, crumbs spilling onto the blanket's blue-and-green weave.

She passed him a plate and filled one for herself. They didn't speak, as if suddenly shy. Neither ate, as if knowing their hunger would not be so easily relieved.

Megan leaned back on her elbows, the sunlight

shifting across her features. "This is the first time I've ever brought anyone here."

"It's beautiful," Gino said.

"There are no diamond trees."

He gave her a rueful smile. "Point taken."

"Did you take all your masters there?" She plucked a grape and rolled it between her thumb and forefinger. "To seduce them?"

Gino was unabashed. "You weren't the first."

"But I'll be the last, won't I?"

"Yes, you will." He took her teasing gaze and turned it solemn.

She looked past him. The sun was halfway toward the horizon. "Are you ready to go home?"

"It's my fate."

It wasn't the answer she'd expected. Would it be easier if he acted as he had before—amusingly anxious for her third wish, offering ludicrous suggestions, urging her on to the point of exasperation? No, nothing would make it easier.

She sensed he was waiting for her reaction, waiting for her to say the things that should not be said. What purpose were pledges of affection, overtures of emotion? Words were not the weapons she needed now. Words were as meaningless as the katydids' constant call. Saying nothing, Megan stood and walked slowly toward the swiftly running stream.

From the grass, he watched her. She was turned toward the sun lowering in the west. Two squirrels chattering above caught her attention. Her head tipped back. Her breasts pushed forward, shaped by the thin fabric of her T-shirt. Gino felt his muscles contract, his throat go dry with longing.

All around them, glazed golden by the setting sun, summer spread her finery. The leaves in the trees above gleamed green and smooth, naively unaware they would soon be no more than a dry rustle underfoot, grieved for only by the boughs left barren. The grass was softer than a newborn's fuzzy cap, only many times longer. But, beneath the down bed beckoning for bodies, there lay the hard, cold earth.

And in their midst, Megan stood posed. Her head angled back, her hair stretching toward her waist, its colors more splendid than the peak plumage of the birds above. She breathed, her breasts barely moving, swelling against cotton. Her weight rested on one leg. The other leg angled in, showcasing a delicate calf perfectly curved and colored by the sun. Her knees met but did not touch. Her thighs were spread slightly as if whispering secrets to each other. Her arms folded across her waist, her fingers curling around her rib cage in an old maid's embrace. She breathed and shifted her weight, causing every perfect part of her to realign. Gino watched in amazement as one masterstroke of movement had created an entirely new, wondrous work of art ready for his eyes to memorize, his senses to immortalize.

MEGAN STOPPED at the water's edge. She heard Gino come up beside her. She didn't look at him.

She'd brought him here to say goodbye. She knew from the beginning, he would leave one day, and it would be she who had set him free. Even knowing that, however, she had foolishly imagined the time would not come so soon. Yet, Fate had conspired against her. It was time for her to break the spell.

While every atom of her being cried otherwise.

She had to let him go, free him of the curse and mortal masters, and so unfettered, triumphantly ascend the steps to his rightful throne. She told herself it was for the best the end came so quickly. She would say it to herself again each morning, when she woke to his image. She would say it at night, as the memory of him put her to sleep. She would repeat it every day for the rest of her life.

But, she would never, ever believe it.

"Gee." Beside her, Gino kicked at a pebble. "I thought this is where you brought all your genie slaves." When she looked at him, his lowered lids lifted just enough to expose the sparkle in his dark eyes. "To seduce them."

She only meant to playfully shove him, but she misjudged the slipperiness of the rocks. She lost her footing and was almost in the water when Gino's hand found hers and pulled her upright.

Their hands clasped, and she steadied herself. They didn't let go. His fingers, his palm lay against her skin in a quiet, concentrated presence. She felt his pulse beating beneath her fingertips with the same steady intensity. Her hand tightened on his.

He started to pull her toward him, she no longer knowing who was the master and who was the slave.

"I didn't know you wanted to go swimming," he

said. Too late she saw that the devilish glint still dominated his eyes.

Before she could get away, he bent and wrapped an arm around her knees. Effortlessly he lifted her and draped her across his shoulder.

"Put me down," she half cried, half laughed as he waded into the water up to his knees.

She pounded on his back, meeting only hard muscle. The stream had reached his thighs, turning his denims black. She felt the water wet her bare feet. The rest of her body knew only the sheer power of the man carrying her.

"No, no," she cried, laughing with such desperate delight, the katydids stopped their song to listen to her strange joy.

"Put me down," she commanded. "No, wait, no, I didn't mean that. I meant—"

The last of her words were lost in a gurgle of water. Just as swiftly, Gino pulled her up and against him, his hands tight on her upper arms.

She flung wet waves of hair out of her face, splattering water across his amused expression.

"I should, I should," she sputtered indignantly.

"What?" he taunted. "What would you like to do to me?"

"This!" She pushed him, the resulting splash music to her ears. He was back on his feet before she was out of reach. As she turned to run away, his arm grabbed hers.

He pulled her close to him once more and through the useless barrier of wet cloth, she felt every long, powerful inch of his body. She pressed against him, her body obeying its own desire strengthened by the sun and the soft breeze and the man washed naked by the rippling water.

This isn't supposed to happen. No good will come of this. Still she lifted her face to him like the summer flowers straining toward the morning sun.

He whispered her name as if it were a prayer. "Megan. Megan." It became a plea, and she heard in his voice the same fear fighting inside her own mind. It was spoken in the last breath on his lips before they came to hers, then fear turned into wonder.

Their mouths mated and spoke, saying silently all the things desired, not even allowed to dream of. Megan's lips opened wider, bidding Gino to enter, to come closer. He answered, his tongue touching hers, exploring the dark, sweetness of her, careful caresses giving way to fierce need.

She clung to him fast like the damp cloth against her body. His touch filled her mouth, her senses, her soul. His hands smoothed her skin, shedding fear and doubt. He touched her everywhere, the dip beneath her earlobe, the cord of her backbone, the slope of her hips. And as he touched her, he took her loneliness with him, clinging to his fingers like cobwebs.

Come inside, her mouth said, separating, seeking him further. Her hands learned the steel line of his neck, as tight as a twist of baling twine. Her fingers crossed to his shoulders, their width filling her palms. She followed the strong, proud square of his back, resting where his spine sunk in a hard hollow, her fingers stopping only briefly before retracing the path they had just forged.

Her tongue followed the line of his teeth, went farther and was stunned by the soft inside of his mouth. Her fingers rose and came home against the contrasting line of his jaw.

He was more than a man. He was magic. She'd seen him rise from nothing more than a cloud; she'd seen him disappear into spaces too small. He would leave her like no other.

Even beneath the molten drape of need and passion, she knew all this. Still, she wrapped her legs around him, her tongue taking his, telling him to touch her, to have her, to come inside. For as much as he belonged to her, she belonged to him.

Carrying her, he started toward the water's edge. She felt the rock of his body against her, and wanted him only, more than anything before or to come. Her legs tightened, her wantonness a revelation, a release. Her mouth held his, their heads moving in a graceful sway, echoing the easy rhythm of Gino's walk, contrasting the beat of two hearts pressed tight.

He laid her on the grass where it was cool in the shade. Then, he stepped back. She looked up at him, seeing that the dimming sun had dropped low beneath his shoulders, reminding her of time's cruel quickness.

She looked up into his eyes, finally admitting to herself what she'd known since the beginning. She loved him with a feeling beyond fairy tales or magic. Her love for him was an emotion past all others, not created by genie powers nor condoned by her pragmatic point of view. Yet, it existed, without mother or father, a power self-sufficient, bestowing wishes not dared to be spoken.

A power demanding she tell Gino the truth now before they went further, before their heedlessness turned this great gift she'd received into no more than a mockery.

He kneeled beside her. His hand traced the oval of her face, the contour of her brow as if she were the supernatural being. His head burrowed lower, his breaths bathing her.

"Gino," she whispered. His fingertips were soft along her body. She saw the throb of life beating in a vulnerable vein along the length of his throat. She pressed her cheek against that thin thread, feeling her tears wetting his skin.

"Megan?" He leaned back, drawing her up with him. The dark desire in his eyes clouded. "What's wrong?"

She couldn't look into those eyes and say the words she knew she must. She looked past him, straight into the traitorous sun, now no more than a haze above the horizon. It was only then she could pass the sentence.

"I'm ready to make the third wish."

Chapter Eleven

"No!" The denial was so full inside him, it took Gino several seconds to realize he'd spoken out loud. Once aware, however, he said it again, one strong syllable of refusal. His gaze lifted, and he was no longer talking to Megan but to the heavens.

Not yet. Tomorrow would be soon enough for her to save the world and he to rule a kingdom. Tonight let him make her happy. His eyes looking upward, he forgot his pride, surrendered his arrogance, presented himself as no more than a humble servant to the powers above One night, he begged. One night, he pleaded.

His gaze found Megan once more. He touched her cheek where a tear had left a trail.

He might not be able to stay with her forever, but let him stay with her tonight. Let him give her his love for this night. For they were here together now, as they should be, as they had to be. *Let it be,* he begged.

His other hand gripping her arm tightened. He wasn't sure what to do, what to say. He didn't know if it was wrong or right. All he knew was he didn't want it to end—not like this with Megan's tears wet on his fingertips.

"No magic tonight," he said, reminding her of her earlier request.

She looked at him, her eyes overly bright with surprise and unshed tears. "You misunderstand," she decided. "I know what I want for the third wish. The last wish."

His hands cupped her face, his eyes inventorying where her pupils lightened and blended into halos mixed green and gold and amber. He made a similar study of her nose, lips, cheeks, brow, hair, simultaneously idolizing and memorizing. Finally he returned to those eyes that had first looked at him three days ago and borne him anew.

He no longer needed the gods and their mercy; he no longer needed a throne and a crown. His heaven, his kingdom began and ended in the woman before him. "Let us have tonight."

In the cradle of his hands, he felt her jaw muscles go slack, then her entire head moved slowly side to side, pressing into one palm, then the other. "Aren't you hearing what I'm saying?"

"Yes." His gaze steadied on her upturned face, stopping its slow swing of confusion, denial.

"You could go home."

There was pain in her eyes when she said the words, the gold tarnishing, the amber dulling to brown.

He bowed his head, kissing lightly, reverently her mouth. Her lips trembled beneath his touch.

"I am home."

New tears fell along her cheeks, as warm as holy water against his fingers.

She came to him, her body as delicate and light as a bud shook free by the first evening breeze. He drew her up, up into his embrace, for the first time in his life, grateful for the humanness he'd been bestowed by birth. Finally freed, it filled his chest, warmed his center, warred with pain, swelled with pleasure.

He clung to her, his hands crushing the thin cotton of her sleeves, and he drank deeply, her sweetness steeping his soul. He wanted to know every inch of her—the hollow below her ear, the frail bone at the back of her knee, the soft billow of flesh where her thigh met her hip. He wanted to gather her hair in both his hands and bring it to his face, rubbing its gentle texture against his brow, his closed lids, the rough, undeserving rounds of his beard until he was washed clean.

It was his newborn heart, which had brought him this far, that stopped him. He pulled back, his body instantly becoming belligerent against the denial. He knew his desire for her would be everlasting, his longing endless. But, no matter, they had been given tonight—one night and nothing more. Except a forever after of pain.

Megan stood before him and even the small space separating them was too much.

"Gino?" she questioned. Her eyes were wide with vulnerability.

"We don't know what we're doing. We're living only in the moment."

"Moments," the least reckless woman he had ever met said, "Moments are all we have."

Her body was motionless as if she'd stopped breathing. But he looked into the fine-lined set of her face and knew if he reached out and touched her chest, he'd find a heart beating as hard as his, its rhythm echoing the same plea he'd offered the gods earlier: *one more night, one more night, one more night.*

"It'll only be for tonight," he had to tell her once more.

She stepped forward, coming back to him like a forgotten dream. "It is more than I ever wished for."

Like the moon calling the tide, they came together. They touched faces, lips, brows above watching eyes, the rushing waters inside them rising, threatening to drown them in desire.

Megan lifted up higher, her mouth following the path blazed by her fingertips. "Gino," she whispered against his parted lips.

With only a taste of his breath, her mouth moved on, savoring the firm warmth of his flesh, the uneven texture of his cheeks. She kissed each eye closed, then her mouth slid down the rough planes of his beard, her tongue scoring a line across his jaw. Her fingers spread across his chest, delighting in the feel of muscle. Her tongue stroked the silken inner curve of his ear. Beneath her hands, she felt his chest swell with a sharp gasp of breath. She pressed her opened mouth to the arc of his neck. She heard a moan, the muscles beneath her fingers went lax.

He gathered her in his arms, drawing her across his thighs, draping her softness across the steel support of his body. Her fingers clung to the bunched muscles of his back. The wide set of his shoulders shielded her from the sun.

Her lips were already opened, waiting for him. His tongue swept their curves, then plunged into the reaches of her mouth, his touch full and fierce, its appetite insatiable.

Her eyes were closed. Too breathless, she couldn't sigh. She didn't hear the groan from the man holding her tightly in his arms. She was deaf, dumb and blind. Her other senses had surrendered to the sensation of touch, the satisfaction of taste.

He pulled her closer, the contours of his chest pressing against the yielding softness of her breasts. Against her, she could feel his hardness, his desire. His tongue probed deeper, sweeping the sensitive insides of her cheeks, its sharp tip savoring the hard ledge across the roof of her mouth. She spread her legs, making a cradle in which her lover lay.

His hands slid down her back in a powerful caress, molding her to him. A pulse began to beat where his thigh met her hip. An echoing ache throbbed deep inside her. Her heart pounded, matching the savage rhythm of his mouth. She opened her lips wider, hungry. She could taste the faint bite of alcohol. She was drunk on the taste and the touch of the man.

His mouth moved away from her lips, kissing the curve of her cheek, the hollow at her temple. He buried his face into the dip of her shoulder, his breath hot on her neck.

''Megan.'' He exhaled as his lips anointed the line of her throat, the length of her hair.

''Gino,'' she answered, her eyes closed, her voice sounding far away. She was spiraling toward oblivion, propelled by the heated movement of Gino's mouth along her throat, across her brow, on each closed eye, each cheek, then finding once more her mouth.

Time fell away. It was no longer day or night, summer or winter. Months had no consequence; years didn't matter. All was darkness and now, defined only by the rhythm of her heart answering Gino's pounding, powerful beat.

Cupping the back of her head, he lifted her up, his mouth never leaving hers. Her back arched, the hardened tips of her breasts rubbing against his chest. He drank deeply, as if he were a depleted man trying to saturate his spirit. Her hips moved against him in a long, slow shiver of need. Her hands found his hair, and she held her mouth to his, drawing him in, bidding him to drink from the wellspring that is woman.

He lifted his head, forcing her to open her eyes. In his eyes, dark with desire, there was a rare light illuminating an emotion so pure, so strong, there could be no doubt as to its name. She reached up her hand and touched his face.

He instinctively turned to the curve of her palm, kissing its soft center. "I love when you touch me," he murmured.

Her other hand came up in response and played across the marble slant of his cheek. She drew his face down to hers, her lips meeting his with reverent desire. His lips parted at her touch. Her tongue searched deep into the dark recesses, suffusing herself with the mystery of man. Her fingers tangled in his hair. Her body pressed unashamedly against him, her blood thick with desire, the thunder inside her, growing louder, blocking out all but the taste of him, the touch of him. Her head fell back, offering him the satin length of her throat. The roar became unbearable. She needed more than the velvet magic of his mouth or the blinding pleasure of his hands as they stroked her hair, her back, the curves of her waist. She needed him inside her, taking away the separateness of their worlds.

"Make love to me," she whispered.

The movement of Gino's mouth stopped. His lips lingered for a forever moment on the slender cord of her neck. Then he pulled away and sat up, his hands still holding the circle of her waist. For one mad minute, she thought he was going to refuse but then, she saw the smoke of desire clouding his eyes, choking his breath.

His head began a dreamlike descent, and unable to wait, she rose to meet him. His answer was the barest touch of his lips grazing the delicate O of her mouth, tormenting her with the mere taste of a kiss. His hands moved slowly from her midriff, up her rib cage, curving around the shape of her breasts beneath the cotton layers.

He pulled her up, gently drawing the T-shirt out of the waistband of her cutoff jeans and up over her head. His hands shaped the bare rounds of her shoulders. His finger traced the naked line of her spine, the soft puffs of flesh at the scalloped edge of her bra. He unhooked the garment in the back, easing down the shoulder straps until the bra fell away. He sat back, admiring her. Her breasts, glazed smooth by the sun's farewell golden light, felt full, heavy. Her nipples were tight, tawny circles.

He gathered her breasts in his hands, holding the weight of them in the warmth of his palms. She arched toward him, giving a breathless cry as his mouth covered one coppery tip, then the other, back and forth, as shooting darts of pleasure fired down her spine. He eased her back onto the grass, his mouth shaping her, suckling her. Her hips rose and moved against him in a primitive dance of passion.

"Please," she groaned as desire mounted.

He sat back up, a fingertip lightly circling the puckered tips of her breasts, brushing the fine down of her abdomen. His head dropped to taste the stretch of her stomach. Down, down his hands rode the curve and line of her bared legs, finding the tender skin behind her knees, the hard point of her ankle. Then, up again, his fingers stroking the frayed edges of her shorts, seeking the flesh underneath. His mouth kissed the soft inside of her thighs. She lifted her hips as he unzipped her shorts, anxious to be rid of heavy denim. He drew down the light cotton of her panties, his mouth kissing a line across her lower abdomen as her hands entangled in his hair and her body squirmed against him. Suddenly his touch left her and, totally naked, a chill washed over her body. She opened her eyes, seeing the sky above shadowed by the coming night. Her gaze dropped, finding Gino, naked also, and she smiled adoringly, delighted by the spans of smooth flesh to taste with wet kisses, to touch with admiring hands. She reached for him.

He came back to her, his weight warm and welcome on her. He kissed her gently, his tongue brushing back and forth, whispering desire across the inviting softness of her lips.

His fingers touched her everywhere, stroking her until, again, she squirmed beneath him, crazy with pleasure, crazed with need. Still he caressed her with a master's patience, the weight and heat of his body blanketing her in warm flesh and hard muscle, his mouth always moving on hers in a slow, persuasive tremble.

Her hands balled up into fists against his back. Her body arched like a bow strung too tight. There was no more thought, only sensation, only his mouth melting against hers, only a sudden soundless gasp of delight as his fingers fondled her, only a need so strong and elemental it had to be met.

She opened herself to him and in the collision of

their flesh, heaven and earth came together. His body plunged deeply into her, his tongue thrust into her quivering mouth. The gentle touches were gone. The movement of his body was fast and hard and full of the passion he had enticingly promised. His tongue drove into her, repeating the same potent rhythm, reaching deeper, hungry for the part of her no man had ever touched. His arms pressed her body against him, carrying her with him as heaven and earth fell away.

She was no more. He was no more. There was only the motion propelling them, hurtling them through the universe. There was only the moment so exquisite and endless, so unbearably brief.

Their cries of passion sounded as pleasure flooded every part of their bodies, jolting their muscles, then leaving them limp, releasing upon them in wave after wave until the two lovers could cry out no more.

They remained still in each other's arms, their mouths opened on each other. Their breaths, ragged and sweet-tasting, were in perfect rhythm. Peace and contentment flowed over them like the evening song of the birds above.

Megan sighed, moving her mouth lazily along Gino's jaw and settling on the smoothness of his throat. Her hands absently stroked his back, combed through his hair. She didn't open her eyes, still lingering in a limbo of ecstasy. Her muscles twitched, remembering the joy.

She heard his sigh. Smiling, she looked up. He

smoothed the hair away from her face, kissed the tip
of her nose.

"Now, I truly believe you've supernatural powers," she teased.

He shook his head, his smile equally affectionate.
"I've never met anyone like you," he said.

She touched his cheek, her smile becoming wistful.
"Hey, that's my line."

She buried her head in his chest, wanting to stay
there forever. She inhaled, memorizing his smell of
exotic winds and far-off places. Her arms tightened
around him, holding fast to this man, who with a slow
blink, could turn into thin air and be gone.

She'd always known one day, he'd go. But now,
she didn't know if she could bear it.

"Megan?" He tucked a finger under her chin and
tipped her face to his. "Are you sorry?"

"Oh, no." The vehemence of her voice gave no
doubt as to her sincerity.

"Are you scared?"

"Yes." Her voice was now small.

He placed his forehead on hers, his eyes big, close,
staring into hers. "It's taken me two thousand years
to find you. How am I ever going to live without you?
I'm terrified beyond belief."

In the distance, she heard the sharp call of an owl
as if reality was trying to intrude.

"We still have tonight," she told him. "Let's go
home."

And they were. The grass beneath Megan's body
became the stuffed cotton of her comforter. The trees

around them were antique white walls; the moon above was replaced by a ceiling fan.

Still in the circle of her arms, Gino gazed down at her. "You have to admit, there're some advantages to sleeping with a genie."

They crawled beneath the cool cotton sheets and held each other. There were a thousand things they wanted to say, needed to say, but words seemed like such poor vehicles. What words could describe the sheer wonder of a woman's mouth glistening with her lover's kisses or the mysterious marvel of a man's collarbone so straight, strong, yet broken as easily as a twig snapped beneath a single footfall? No words could equal the blending of their beings, the melting of their mortal skins, the marrying of their immortal souls. How could they express the joy, the bliss, even the terror? Silently they clung to each other.

Slowly the gentle strokes turned to longer, deeper caresses. The kisses continued, finding soft spans of flesh to explore, new stretches of skin to christen. Words weren't necessary as the lovers spoke their own language, the banked fires flaring, the gentleness giving way to elemental passion, and the true joy of life found in another's barest touch.

They stayed in each other's arms all night, and if they slept, it was only to dream of the other. Megan awoke as the first gray finger of dawn sliced through the room. The night was over. Morning had come.

Gino's arm and leg made a clumsy arabesque across her body, his limbs heavy and comforting.

She watched him sleep, marveling at the miracle of

two eyes, a nose, a mouth. She kissed the air above his lips, not wanting to waken him. He slept deeply, his breaths full and long.

He'd said it would be easier in the morning to grant the last wish. She'd naively agreed, thinking in the bright, stark light of day, she could be brave.

She wasn't. The coming light only too clearly outlined her lover's proud brow, the black cap of his crown, the sensual shape of his mouth. She wouldn't be able to say goodbye in the day, the bright sun mocking the gray cloud closing over her heart. She wouldn't be able to say goodbye in the night when darkness dropped, laughing at her tears and fears.

I've one wish left, she thought with a possessed woman's greed. *I'll wish to wake every day with his kiss on my brow. To sleep each night, his words of love whispering in my ear.*

Yet, even as she plotted, she knew it wasn't possible. Her last wish belonged to the people at Crelco.

Ashen-faced, Arnold had come into Q.C. yesterday from the department heads' meeting. Crelco had been sold to a rival company in North Carolina, he'd said in a flat monotone. The new company only wanted Crelco's customers. The plant would close in ninety days. Arnold had shaken his head, saying the company president had broken down and cried like a baby when he delivered the news, but the stockholders were holding firm. The official announcement was to be made today. Then, Arnold had sat the rest of the afternoon staring at the blank screen on his computer.

Even if the jobs of her friends, her colleagues

weren't at stake, she still couldn't wish for Gino to stay. Not that she didn't want him to stay. She did—more than life itself. But he had given her happiness. She couldn't ask him to give up his. She looked at the man sleeping so peacefully beside her.

"I love you, Gino." Her voice barely reached a whisper. "If we only had one minute of complete happiness together, the moment, the memory would live forever inside me. Yet, you gave me hours, days—"

Her voice broke. She rolled away from him, her forearm covering her face, ashamed of her own tears, her own cowardice, her own greed. How was she ever going to live without him?

She forced herself to get up and go toward the bathroom. It was just another day, she told herself. She'd take a shower, go to work, come home, have dinner, save a company, then say goodbye to the only man she'd ever love. Tomorrow, and each day after that, she'd rise again, not thinking farther than each forced step.

She almost made it to the bathroom door before turning and finding her way back into the warm bed. She slipped effortlessly into the waiting circle of his arms, then cried soundlessly on his chest as the morning grew lighter and he slept unaware.

GINO SLEPT for the first time in four days. He slept so long and soundly that when he woke he was completely disoriented. While he stretched like a lion with a full belly, his eyes scanned the brown walls circling him. Slowly memory returned. He remembered last night. He remembered loving Megan. He loved her still. He'd love her always.

She must not have wanted to wake him when she left for work in the morning. As soon as she was over five hundred feet away, he'd been returned to the crock pot.

He stretched again, almost fully awake and aware of a gnawing in the pit of his stomach. Another day, it would be hunger. But he'd known hunger, and this sensation was sharper, more piercing. He sat up now, completely conscious.

He'd been alone his entire life, but, for the first time, he knew what it was like to feel loneliness. He also knew the ache would now be his constant companion unless Megan was by his side.

BY THE TIME MEGAN finally forced herself to leave the house, she was already an hour late for work. When she entered the plant, she saw the shell-shocked expressions of her co-workers, their motions more mechanical than usual as the endless parade of parts climbed up the conveyor belts, then fell into heavy plastic bins with the regularity of a death knell. She knew the announcement had been made. Wanda came toward her, the old woman's face more tightly lined than usual. She looked at Megan with a vacant stare.

"I know," Megan mouthed against the heartless clatter and clash of the presses.

She wondered how Elliot had taken the news. A stony stare he'd given her when they'd passed in the plant had been their only communication since the night at Kitty's. She had tried to talk to him once in the warehouse, but he'd only stepped too hard on the pedal of the forklift and gone whizzing down the aisle, nearly knocking over a skid of wire spools that were seven feet high.

She had decided then he needed a little more time to cool off, but she wanted to go to him now and explain he didn't have to worry. She knew he needed the support of a friend right now. No matter what had happened between them, she wanted to be that friend.

She saw him through the wide glass windows of the recycling supervisor's office. He was standing by his boss's desk, separating invoices. She was glad to see he was alone.

She knocked lightly on the door and entered. "Hi." It came out a squeak. She closed the door behind her but kept one hand on its knob. "How's it going?"

He glanced at her before continuing to concentrate on the piles of thin slips across the desk. Still Megan had seen the flash of surprise before his face had become curtained with cold pride.

"What do you want?" His voice was toneless.

"I wanted to see, that is, make sure, you're okay." She fumbled for the right words.

He briefly looked at her again then went back to the piles he was creating. "I'm fine."

She focused on the swift motion of the papers being sorted, trying to figure out what to say.

He paused, granting her a condescending look. "Was there something else?"

"I wanted to tell you, well, I thought you might be worried." She took a tentative step toward the desk. "And I just wanted to say, you don't have to."

"I don't have to what?" Elliot asked in his trademark tone of endless patience.

"Worry," she blurted. "You don't have to worry."

"Well, thank you." His tone turned sarcastic. "I won't now."

She moved closer, wanting to make him understand. "What I mean is, the plant hasn't closed yet."

He looked up at her sharply before the mask of indifference could fall on his emotions. She saw anger so deep it made her step back.

"Anything could happen between now and ninety days." She smiled encouragement.

"Of course. How did I forget?" Elliot slapped his forehead, his expression again sublimely sufferable. "You—" he pointed a finger at her "—have the genie."

She stopped smiling.

"And you've another wish left, don't you?" He was now smiling, the curl of his mouth too broad.

Megan stared down at the desk, away from Elliot's sneering gaze.

"This is great." He rounded the desk and pulled out the chair, aiming it toward her. "Sit down. C'mon. Sit down." His voice took on a manic tone.

She slowly sat down. She'd made a mistake coming here.

He pushed her behind the desk. "Here's a pad and

a pen." He stood behind her. "We'll compose a memo. After all, why should anyone worry? How should we begin? I mean, do you want to go all the way back to the crock pot, or can we skip the background and bring on Ali Baba?"

She started to get up.

"Sit." Behind her, Elliot put his hand on her shoulder and pushed her down. He spun the chair so she faced him. He gripped the chair arms and leaned down, close to her face.

"Don't you understand, Megan? You're sick. Kimberly called it delusional. You need help—professional help. Kimberly's specialty isn't psychiatry, but she's done a rotation in the area. She's offered to talk to you."

"Kimberly?" Megan asked. "Your old girlfriend?"

Elliot straightened. "We had dinner together last night. No big deal."

The flush creeping up the stiff edge of his collar said otherwise.

"Just two old friends getting together," he went on. "Talking about old times."

"And your psychotic ex-fiancée," Megan added.

He visibly bristled. "What would you've preferred? That I told you Kimberly floated into my bedroom in a bubble like Glenda the Good Witch?"

Megan smiled. "Elliot, you naughty boy."

His flush turned magenta. "Don't make light of this. You're sick."

She swiveled back to the front of the desk. "Actually I've never felt better.'' She was about to stand up when the black, bold letters ACK on an invoice stopped her.

Elliot was saying something else, but she wasn't listening. She was reading the bill on the top of the stack, then she read the one below it, and the one below that.

''Elliot.'' She stopped him midsentence. She stood up, clutching the thin sheets of paper. ''What are these?''

Chapter Twelve

Elliot took the bills from her hand. "These are the monthly charges for ACK disposal." He threw the papers back on the desk. "Now, as I was saying, Kimberly could refer—"

"ACK disposal?" Megan asked.

Elliot's features pulled tight. "Are you listening to me? I'm trying to help you."

"What ACK disposal?"

The long-suffering expression returned. "A waste-hauling company from Canada gets rid of ACK and our other hazardous materials. It costs Crelco big bucks, but we can't just dump the stuff on the ground."

Megan looked down at the papers, then back up at Elliot. "But we are."

"What're you talking about?"

"There's a pit out behind the plant. I saw them dumping tankers of ACK only three days ago."

Elliot's eyes narrowed. "You were in the pit behind the factory three days ago? Why?"

Megan shifted her weight. "Actually it was Gino

and me. We had to find his crock pot. Remember, I'd asked you if I could put it in a company garbage bin? That was before I knew—"

Elliot's laughter cut her off. "Why am I wasting my time? If you want help, come see me." He started toward the door.

Megan gathered the invoices in her hand. "Don't you think someone should know?"

He stopped at the door. "What are you talking about?"

She gestured with the bills tight in her fist. "Isn't illegal dumping a federal offense?"

"What're you saying?" Elliot asked, his back still turned to her.

"If the new company finds out about the contamination, they might back out of the deal." Megan's voice became excited. "Crelco could stay open."

Elliot turned around. "Not after they dished out the millions of dollars for cleanup costs, not to mention the fines. The EPA doesn't fool around anymore. They're putting people in jail for illegal dumping. Do you really think anyone would take that kind of risk?"

The excitement withdrew from Megan's expression. The determination stayed. "Whether Crelco stays open or not, somebody should know."

Elliot stepped toward her. "Yes, you could call the new owners' CEO and board of directors. And call Crelco's board, too. Maybe the newspapers, maybe *Sixty Minutes*. Tell them all how you were looking for your genie's crock pot and stumbled onto a hazardous waste area. Better yet, why don't you and your genie just wave a wand. The new owners will disappear, and everything'll be back to normal. Wouldn't that be easier?''

''That was my original plan,'' Megan murmured as she riffled through the stacks of invoices, looking for other ACK disposal bills.

Elliot threw his arms up in the air. ''What happened to the rational, reasonable woman I proposed to?'' he asked.

Megan smiled. She knew exactly what had happened to her: Gino.

''Do you want to go out to the dump site with me?'' she asked.

Mouth open, Elliot looked at her. ''You're serious.''

''I know these papers here say ACK is being shipped to Canada for legal disposal, but I also know Sunday afternoon, Gino and I watched tankers dump the same material not half a mile from where you're standing right now. The new owners aren't going to want that liability. Crelco will have to stay open to pay cleanup costs.

''It makes perfect sense,'' Elliot agreed.

''You think so?'' The excited tone came back into Megan's voice.

''Absolutely. The DEC has even recently begun giving polluters a break. They're finding if the company closes down because of huge fines and cleanup costs, there's still the problem of the contamination site. It's a lose-lose situation.''

"Do you think Crelco would be eligible for assistance?"

"Why not? All you have to do is explain to the Federal government how you and the genie who lives in your crock pot are trying to save the company and protect the community from a miniature Love Canal in their backyard."

The hope that had illuminated Megan's features switched off.

"Now," Elliot said as if talking to a child, "let me have those papers, please. Thank you."

He stacked the bills neatly before inserting them into a folder. "I want you to forget all this nonsense. Why don't you let me call Kimberly right now? You could talk to her on the phone, maybe make plans to meet her after work."

Megan watched Elliot even up another pile of papers. Gino had been right. Elliot was never going to believe in something that didn't make sense. She couldn't blame him. As a matter of fact, not more than four days ago, she probably would have reacted the same way.

"Thanks, Elliot, but I've got something to do after work today."

IT WAS PAST DINNERTIME before Megan finally burst through the back door of the house. There was no need to call for Gino. He was already there, his arms crushing her to his body.

"Where were you?" he demanded, his mouth making a quick slide over her forehead, her hair, her cheek. "Why didn't you call?"

"I didn't know the crock pot had a cellular," she teased before his mouth covered hers, and her body went heavy with desire.

He'd been in her thoughts all day, but her thoughts were mere mental alms compared to the touch of him, the smell of him, the tremble of his body as it met hers once more. How would she ever say goodbye to him?

She clung to him tighter, her mouth opened in welcome, moaning with desire, her legs wrapping around his waist when he lifted her and carried her toward the bedroom.

They made it as far as the couch. There was lust and hunger and passion and love, most of all, love. There was love in the way his hand found hers, their fingers interlacing, love in the reverent murmur of her name, the support of the pillow he propped behind her head. There was love as he watched her, matching his body's movements to her expressions until together, they rode as one to realms Megan had before denied in her dreams.

Afterward, they rested in each other's arms, the clock on the mantel counting the passing seconds out loud. Megan sought solace in the information she'd discovered today, knowing she'd bargained them extra time. But how long? Ten minutes? Ten days? Ten thousand years? And still, she'd feel cheated.

"You were gone when I woke this morning," Gino

said pointedly. He pulled her up, draping her across him, bringing her mouth to his.

"You were sleeping so soundly, I didn't want to wake you." Her kisses along his jawline were lighter than the flutter of fairies' wings.

"Then, you were late coming home."

She lingered on the muscled length of his neck, the brittle strength of his collarbone, impressing it on her memory. "I had to run an errand."

"I don't know why you left at all." His hands played along her back, passing across the hollow where the muscles softened and spread to the fullness of her buttocks.

"I'm a coward." She caught his earlobe in her teeth and tugged on it gently before whispering into the opening above, "Make love to me again."

They did, with a desperate tangling of limbs and a fierce, aching passion. They called out to each other as if Fate had already separated them. Then, their cries became one voice celebrating ecstasy, damning sorrow, daring to even challenge Fate.

Afterward, they lay content and too heavy to move. Gino lazily stroked her hair. "Megan?"

"Mmm?" she murmured.

"The third wish?"

She lifted her head, meeting the depths of his black eyes. There, she saw the same fear, the same sadness she'd struggled with all day.

"Are you sure it's what you want?" he asked.

"What I want," she said, her expression openly pained, "is time. Time for us to be together."

Gino smiled, then kissed her lightly on the lips. "That is yours without wishing."

"But once I make my last wish, you're gone...forever."

He studied her, the relief in his face once more giving way to worry. "You want time, but you must wish for something else?"

"They're closing down Crelco," she said.

Comprehension came into his expression, turning it sober. "You want to save the company."

Megan nodded.

He sat up. "Then, time, a capricious creature at best, is no longer ours." He stood and circled the room.

"Not necessarily," Megan suggested.

He stopped, midstep. "Attempt to outwit the very force that brought me here? No, Ishtar herself would snatch me from your arms, then work her own wrath upon your world."

"What if we don't use the third wish to save Crelco?"

Gino looked at her, puzzled. "Use ordinary means?"

Megan jumped up from the couch. "Wait here. I've got something to show you."

When she came back into the room, she was holding a long, clear cylinder sealed in a plastic bag. She told Gino about meeting with Elliot, the waste-hauling company, the dangers of ACK contamination.

She held up the oblong canister. "The Cooperative Extension agent showed me how to use this to take a soil sample. If we can prove the land behind Crelco is contaminated, the sale will be off. The Co-op agent also told me, state funding has been made available to help with environmental clean-ups in an effort to encourage new businesses or keep current businesses from going under.''

Gino looked at the plastic tube in Megan's hand.

She went to him. "I know we can't have forever. I don't even know if we'll have tomorrow. We might only get an hour, a minute. Still it's one minute less I'll have to live without you.''

He smiled as he reached for her hand. "What've we got to lose? Let's go.''

THERE WAS NO MOON in the sky. Only darkness altering the strange shapes of the dump. There were no sounds, only an unnatural stillness, amplifying the rhythmic breath of the intruders.

"Should I go ahead and check for rats?" Megan teased, her voice sounding too loud in the quiet. She arced the flashlight beam across the uneven landscape of trash.

"Snakes, too," Gino, at her side, suggested.

"Snakes?" She turned the light, catching Gino's smile.

"Don't worry. I doubt they're poisonous.''

"Okay," Megan conceded. "I deserve that." She stepped toward the dump. The night air was warm and close. Still she shivered. "Let's get the soil sample, and get out of here.''

The air seemed suddenly heavy, weighted with an

acrid smell that clung to her skin and made her breaths shallow.

"Do you smell that?" she asked Gino.

He nodded. "Eau de ACK?"

Megan reached her hand out for the container Gino was carrying. She gave him the flashlight.

"It hasn't rained so we can take the sample from just below the surface," she said, ripping open the plastic bag.

She knelt down. "If they're dumping those chemicals out here," she said, "I'd like to know why a waste-hauling company in Canada is being paid thousands of dollars."

"Who's paying them?" Gino asked.

Megan twisted off the container's cover. "Crelco, of course."

"Who specifically hired the waste-hauling company?"

Megan stopped, midscoop. "What?"

"Who's submitting the bills to Crelco's accounts department to be paid?"

Megan looked up at Gino, seeing only the glare of the flashlight full on her face. He moved the beam out of her eyes. She blinked several times. Slowly her pupils dilated, restoring her vision. She saw Gino's face above her. In her mind's eye, she saw something else: Elliot's initials at the bottom of each of the billing invoices.

"Gino?" Out of her peripheral vision, she saw a bright light, dismissing it as an aftereffect of her momentary blindness. Then, the light was full on Gino, illuminating his face, his body. She saw the lips she should have never kissed, yet had welcomed hers so tenderly. She saw the proud, solid stance that she'd learned could soften and curl around another like a cocoon. In that flash of brilliant light, she saw and remembered everything of the man she loved. She couldn't breathe, so complete was her awe.

There was a tremendous explosion. She was hurling through the air, not carefully like when Gino had carried her to the clouds above. No, she was being thrown without care or reason as if she was no more than the trash piled not far from where she just stood.

She landed hard on the ground, heard several snaps like slim sticks being broken in two. Pain careened through her body like a runaway roller coaster. Everything was black. Her only awareness was pain. She could smell the sickeningly sweet scent of blood and realized it was her own. It came wet and sticky down her face until she could taste it.

Inside her, she screamed, "Gino!"

But when she spoke out loud, the sound did not even reach a whisper.

"Gino." It was no more than a breath.

Yet, her heart still beat, calling to him, crying his name. Each throb of blood pumped it through her veins, spilled it out onto her flesh. With his name pulsing in her ears, she wiped the blood from her eyes with her left hand. Her right arm wouldn't move. She wiped again, through the smoke, seeing small fires scattered around her, feeling their heat sear her skin, the smoke choking her.

Not far, ten feet, she saw him, a lifeless outline flattened against the ground, his limbs twisted unnaturally around him.

"Gino," she barely whispered, crawling toward him, her right side dragging beneath her, her vision now clouded with tears. She no longer felt pain or the rough unyielding ground beneath her as she went inch by inch to the man she loved.

She had no idea how long it took. One foot closer seemed an eternity. Time slowed, matching the crippled movement of her body. Halfway there, she collapsed, panting heavily. Her head fell to the dirt, the gritty taste of soil mixing with the sweetness of blood.

She heard a soft, anguished moan. She lifted her head to see Gino stir, his left hand stretching out, reaching toward her.

He was alive. Strength flowed back into her bones, broken or whole. She began her lopsided sidle once more, her own hand leading, grasping fistfuls of dirt and debris, extending full-length toward Gino.

Their fingers touched first. She felt the false resilience of his human flesh, and a sob left her body like the wind leaving a sail. She began to cry harder.

"Megan?"

"I'm here." She brought her body closer to his, mindful of the strange setting of his legs and arms, fearful of causing him more pain. She stretched alongside him, the image of them lying like this first as lovers flashing into her mind. Now, his body was so cold.

"The wish," he not more than mouthed to her.

The wish. Joy filled her as if her body had already been healed. The wish.

"I wish," she said before Gino was forced to feel another millisecond of pain, "for our lives."

She waited, serene in the knowledge her wish would be granted.

She saw Gino close his eyes. One minute, two minutes.

Nothing happened.

Gino opened his eyes. He opened his mouth as if to speak, but, only a tiny bubble of blood appeared, then popped.

"What's wrong? Why didn't it work?"

She moved up closer to him to lessen the strain of speech.

"I'm too weak. I've lost too much of my power. I can't save both of us."

He paused, the words he spoke taking their toll.

He closed his eyes, gathering strength. His eyes opened. "I can only save one of us." Even as weak as he was, she could feel the strength in his words: "Save yourself, Megan."

She looked into his eyes. Her voice was low, but empowered with a sudden calm. "You've already given me more than I dared wish for."

He tried to shake his head. She saw the stab of pain stopping his movement.

"Shh." She stroked his hair. The blood was already beginning to dry. "Don't try to move. Don't try to talk."

He looked at her, and she saw love—the love he'd never spoken of, but she sensed was there.

He raised a hand, its pointed finger trembling. He pointed to her, then he pointed to his heart.

"You told me genies couldn't give love." She was smiling. "I told you I didn't need love. We were wrong, weren't we?"

"Wish for life, Megan." His whisper was willed with the fleeting remnants of his strength.

He kissed the quieting finger she placed against his lips.

"You've given me my happiness, Gino."

She leaned down and kissed his lips, which were moist with blood.

"Now it's time I give you yours."

His hand on hers suddenly tightened with a surprising force of strength, causing her to open her eyes and meet the light of command not yet taken from his dark pupils.

"Wish for life, Megan," his whisper demanded.

She closed her eyes once more, kissing one last time his lips.

"I wish for life." A final kiss before she whispered against his open mouth, "Your life."

Chapter Thirteen

"No-o-o-o-o!"

The scream started inside him as all turned blackness. He felt himself lifted, flying through dimensions. The scream gained strength until it was a loud wail echoing through time and space.

The darkness parted as if sliced neatly down the middle by his scream. He was in the Great Forest. His form was restored to its original health. All physical pain and weakness was gone.

He stopped his cries, silenced by the eerie quiet. He waited.

"Gilgamesh, you were so close," said the voice that had cursed him two thousand years ago.

He spun around, meeting Ishtar, who was resplendent in golden robes, her beauty otherworldly. Time hadn't touched her.

"Tell me." She leaned forward, the force of her handsome features mesmerizing. "How does it feel to be so close to the thing you desire most..." She measured with her hands. "And have it slip through

your fingers?'' She rubbed her hands together as if
scattering ashes.

He looked into those feline eyes and knew she
wasn't talking about the throne.

"Why am I alive?" he demanded.

"Isn't that what your last master wished for?"

"I didn't grant that wish."

"Yes, I know." Ishtar clucked her tongue. The
sound lifted and echoed among the trees like a tolling
bell. "You didn't fulfill the terms of the curse." She
traced the slant of his cheekbone with a pointed crim-
son fingernail. "Pity."

He grabbed her hand, twisting it at the wrist. "Is
she alive?"

Ishtar's hand slipped from his, and she was gone.

"That's not what she wished for, is it?" The taunt
came from behind him.

He spun around. The goddess floated before him.

"Did she live?" His demand was anguished.

Ishtar rose, her hair billowing in light waves. "You
failed, Gilgamesh," she sentenced him.

"Let her live, Ishtar."

He struggled to rise. Nothing happened.

Laughing, she looked down at him. "Twist and
turn until you're coiled like the serpent Sinbad met
on his third voyage. It doesn't matter. Your powers
are gone. You're no more than a mortal."

He looked up at the specter streaming golden. She
was smiling, preparing to enjoy his reaction. He
looked down at his own form. He was a man.

So, it was done. And it mattered not at all—the

loss of his powers, the theft of the throne. All that mattered was saving Megan's life. A singular determination steadied him. "A mortal man won't survive long in these tiers. Show mercy, and bring death to me swiftly. Surely my death will suffice for the mortal woman's soul. Let her live."

Ishtar descended slowly to the ground. "Twice you've sacrificed your life for this woman."

"If I had two thousand lives to give, they would all be hers."

Level with him now, the goddess gazed at him. The gold lace that was draped high across her bosom evenly rose and fell.

"Do my eyes deceive me? My ears prove false? Is this the Gilgamesh who would not satisfy a goddess's desire and refused the riches of the high heavens above? Yet now you freely surrender your throne, your powers, your very life? And for what?"

"For Megan," the mortal man replied calmly.

"Is she a sorceress, a she-devil, a siren?" Ishtar challenged.

"She is a woman. Let her live."

Ishtar tipped her head, and the sun in the sky above became the cool eye of the moon. "You amuse me, Gilgamesh. Normally your disobedience would earn you death, but my good mood gives way to generosity. You will be banished."

"Do what you will with me. Send me straight to Hell, if you must, but save Megan."

"You'll go to a sphere of sadness and trouble, tribulations and toil."

"Send me now, this second, before death comes any closer to the woman who waits in the world below."

"Gilgamesh." Ishtar's hand took his, her flesh as cool and smooth as ivory. "I can never say goodbye to you without great regret. Yet, I don't doubt you will cross my path again. Until then, I will miss you. You were unique among the Jinn."

"My heritage predicted my place. My mother's mortal genes made me what I was."

"They would've destroyed a lesser being. In you, they became a cause for celebration. You believed your mother cursed you, but you were blessed at birth. And in the end, the curse will come around and become a blessing."

"You speak in riddles, Goddess. Come clear."

"The answer is inside you, Gilgamesh." She laid a hand on his chest. "It's always been inside you. You'll not disappoint me." She arced her arms to send him away.

"Wait. Answer one riddle before I go, or I'll forever wander in uneasy exile."

Ishtar dropped her arms.

"Does Megan live or die?"

Ishtar smiled. "You have the answer. It's inside you."

"No, no." Desperation made his voice tremble. "No more games."

"Shh. Calm yourself. Close your eyes, and let me whisper the answer against those lips more tempting than Eden's fruit."

He did as she asked, feeling a cool brush of flesh against his, hearing the words whispered, "Look inside yourself." Then, there was nothing.

"Did she live?" He had to know.

He opened his eyes. Ishtar was gone. All was darkness again.

"No-o-o-o-o!" The scream that had brought him back to this universe carried him back out.

"Gino? Gino?"

Someone was shaking him, calling his name. He opened his eyes, banishing the blackness. His pupils focused, seeing Kitty, her face floating above him.

"They said one person could go in now."

He immediately sat up, aware of everything—the slick pull of vinyl upholstery against his clothes, the walls of innocuous beige with interchangeable floral prints. The carpet was a deeper bland hue, muffling the quick footsteps of people passing by, many of them dressed in white or equally colorless tones.

"I wanted to go, but I think it should be you." Kitty's smile was betrayed by the worry pinching her features. Her eyes were puffy as if tender to the touch.

He stood up, the fluorescent lights above casting an unreal sheen on the surroundings. Everything seemed too clear and transparent as he'd imagined in a dream scene. Genies didn't fall prey to the dream demons, but, he knew too well, mortals did. Mortals such as he.

A woman in white led him down a long hall. The low whoosh of machines circled all around him, soft and rhythmic as embryonic breath. He followed the straight-seamed steps of the woman leading him.

"I hope none of the reporters got to you. We're trying our best to keep them away. They're all dying for a statement from you on Elliot's arrest," the woman said.

Gino stopped, looking up from the rubber heels to the no-nonsense set of the woman's back. "What?"

The woman kept walking in staccato time as if she hadn't heard him. By the time Gino caught up with her, she was saying, "All those months, he'd been charging Crelco for hauling chemicals, but dumping everything in the backyard. I heard on the noon report a few other guys and some old marine buddy who worked at a Canadian company were sharing in the take, but supposedly, as ring leader, Elliot was getting the bulk of it. They're talking jail time, being he set the explosion and all."

"Elliot?" Gino said.

"Hard to believe, huh? He claims he was only trying to get rid of evidence." The woman in white stopped before a closed door. "Tell that to his ex-fiancée in there." The woman opened the door.

He saw Megan and forgot all else. He looked at her and felt not the joy he'd expected but dark, convulsing pain. She lay on the bed, a sheet pulled up to her bare shoulders. Tubes ran out of her mouth, her nose, and her one arm exposed above the line of the sheet, looking especially disembodied and helpless.

He stepped toward her. She was so still, somewhere between life and death.

"There's been no change in the last seventy-two hours." The woman in white was straightening tubes, checking wires, fiddling with buttons. "But it's a miracle she's even alive after the blast she took."

He stood beside the bed, looking down at her. She was motionless, her skin as white as the bedclothes except for the bruises contrasting purple. He pulled up a chair and sat down beside her. He reached out, wanting to take her hand. It was so small, a narrow tube strapped to its backside. He didn't want to hurt her.

"Go ahead," the woman in white said. He'd forgotten she was there. "Touch her. Talk to her."

He lifted the hand, which was as light as a leaf.

"And Gino?" The unexpected sound of his name drew his attention to the woman who had brought him here. "I won't be far."

He saw Ishtar's face, then the woman vanished.

"Ishtar," he called. "Come back." He looked down at Megan, the delicately drawn blue veins along her closed eyelids. "Help me," he said in a quieter voice.

He laid his forehead on the bed, unable to bear the sight of Megan so lifeless, so helpless, suspended between Heaven and Earth. Her hand laid in his, cool, inert, unresponsive.

"Hell would've been easier, Ishtar," he murmured. His frustration and fear ballooned into fury. His head reared up not unlike a caged animal.

"Punish me," he railed against the air. "But let her live."

His pleas met silence.

He gazed wildly around the room, the blank walls seeming to come closer, the lingering smell of disinfectant making him nauseous. One of the machines above the bed monitoring Megan's vitals flashed a steady seventy. Another screen kitty-corner showed a series of small blips. He stared at them, seeing what it meant to be mortal.

He fought back the hopelessness rising like a black swell and trying to carry him away. Not yet. Not while Megan's heart still beat.

His genie powers were gone. He had only mortal magic now. He knew it existed. As a genie, his human instincts had felt it, been drawn to it. It was this elusive yearning that had stood him separate from his own kind. He'd thought it a curse.

Could it now be a blessing?

You believed your mother cursed you, but you were blessed at birth.

"What was I blessed with?" he asked the nothingness.

All was still, punctuated only by the rhythmic, electronic beat of Megan's heart as if it were a perverse lullaby. Then, the numbers on the screen began to drop—seventy, sixty-seven, sixty-five. Gino stood up and ran to the hallway, the sounds of his pleas preceding him: "Help me. Help me."

He jerked back the door, meeting only white fog without floor or ceiling. There was no one, nothing. He drew back.

The numbers were still dropping, the blips barely existent.

"Don't die, Megan." He went to her and picked up her hand, its skin as white as wax. His gaze darted around the room. There was no one, but Megan and he. He was the only one who could save her.

But how? How? he mutely screamed. What was the answer? He could barely feel her frail pulse. His prayers became frenzied.

The answer is inside you.

He shook his head. Any answers he'd ever had were within the woman now lying so unnaturally still before him. All he had inside him now was a feeling for her so powerful, so large, it took his breath away each time he looked at her.

The answer is inside you.

If he was a doctor, a nurse, even a faith healer, he might know.

But he was, now, no more than a man.

And it was as a man, he knelt down, bowed his forehead and laid his cheek against his beloved's and uttered the single sentence more powerful, more extraordinary than any feat ever accomplished with his supernatural abilities.

"I love you, Megan."

And in a heartbeat, Gino became one with mortal magic.

He felt a twitch against his cheek, so slight he was afraid he'd imagined it. But when he lifted his head, he saw a small spasm beneath Megan's closed left eye. He bent down and kissed the soft spot where the muscle had moved.

He felt another flutter against his cheek and was certain he could feel no greater joy. He was proved wrong when he lifted his head and saw it had not been another muscle twitch summoning him, but the caress of an eyelash lifting.

Megan looked up at him. Her hand rose and went to his cheek, his brow, his lips. The tubes were gone, and there was a glow in her eyes belying the injuries she'd suffered. She smiled, once more touching his hair, his face.

He turned blindly into her palm, kissing its velvet plain. Her fingers curled around his cheek. Her mouth moved, working at first without sound. He bent down to her, and two words rose to meet him as delicately as life's first breath:

"Hi, Elvis."

Relief rolled into his body, making his muscles weak. He laid his cheek against Megan's, his tears becoming hers. All that had almost come to pass welled within him. His shoulders shuddered like a wave breaking, and he clung to her as if he'd lose her again. He felt the circle of her arms, smelled the sweetness of her flesh, felt the softness of her hair, and the wave broke, convulsing his body with sobs.

She slid her face through the wetness and found his mouth. She soothed him, gently stroking his back, his shoulders. The salt of their tears was eclipsed by the perfume of her breath, the delicate press of her mouth. He closed his eyes and calmness came.

If he was asked how long the kiss continued, he wouldn't know. If he was asked to describe the touch of her lips to his, the sweet melding of their mouths, the heady taste of her breath bringing life to his starved soul, he wouldn't be able to find the words. All he knew when their mouths separated, and he could still feel the smile of her lips, was that the curse was over.

He held tight the woman he loved and came home.

"What happened, Gino?" she asked him.

He told her about his return to the Upper Realms, the meeting with Ishtar, the loss of his genie self.

"You're a human now? Just like me?"

He smiled lovingly at her. "I still sport a few different parts."

He watched, certain his own joy would only be magnified by her features. Instead he saw her brows beetle. Worry lines wrinkled the bridge of her nose. He became alarmed. "You're disappointed?"

"No, no." Yet pain tensed her expression. "But I wished for your life?"

He smiled once more, drawing her to him and kissing her lips, pulled tight with worry. "And now, I have my life."

"But your throne? Your powers? Your dream?"

"What good is a throne without a queen? What use were all my powers if I couldn't love? I have no dream but you, Megan."

"You sacrificed everything?"

"I sacrificed nothing."

The tightness was easing away from her mouth.

Still she protested. "But, you said you couldn't save us both? Your powers weren't strong enough."

"My genie powers weren't strong enough. But I have new powers now, human powers that derive their strength from the single greatest source of power known to man—love. It was that power that saved you...and me. I love you, Megan."

She listened to what he said, her lips now lax with wonderment. He saw the same awe in her eyes as she tangled her hands in his hair and drew his head down in a dreamlike descent.

"I love you, Gino."

She kissed him as if tasting him for the first time, the caress of her tongue, the press of her body mutely beckoning. She held fast to him, their mouths moving in a rhythmic give and take, the kiss deepening into a dance without leads, her whispered words of affection met with his replies until all that surrounded them was the repeated joy of love.

Neither was aware of the nurse at the door until they heard: "You're awake? And already participating in physical therapy?"

The lovers looked up. Megan's lips were full and fat from Gino's kisses, the flush on her skin speaking not embarrassment but happiness.

Sunlight angled across the doorway, allowing Gino to see only a female figure outlined in white.

The nurse walked briskly into the room, Megan's open chart in her hand. The sun's glare still obscured her face. She turned to lower the shade against the strong light, and Gino saw the long strand of white-blond hair that had worked its way loose from beneath her cap. He got up.

The nurse was turning toward Megan as Gino rounded the bed.

"Miss Kelly, I don't see a doctor's order discontinuing your IV? Who took your tubes out?" she demanded.

"You did, Ishtar." Gino grabbed the nurse by the shoulders, turning her toward him. "Now let me give you a great, big, wet..." He was stopped by the stranger's face before him.

"A great, big, wet what, Sir?" the nurse asked, setting down Megan's chart and folding her arms beneath a sturdy bosom.

Megan giggled. The nurse turned back toward the bed, warily watching Gino from the corner of her eye.

"Miss Kelly, you've taken a miraculous turn for the better." She took Megan's arm and held it firmly at the wrist to check her pulse. "Still, let's move a little slower down the road to recovery." She counted the seconds on her oversize wristwatch. "That means not removing your tubes and restricting activity with your..." She sent Gino a disapproving look. "Friend."

She dropped Megan's wrist, and lifting the sheet halfway, rolled her with automatic movements to one side, then the other. When she was finished, the nurse folded her arms once more beneath her breasts, sucked in her cheeks and looked down at Megan.

"I'm going to get the doctor," she pronounced.

"Is something wrong?" Megan and Gino both asked.

"No, nothing's wrong."

"So, that's good?" Gino said.

The nurse turned at the door. "That's impossible."

Gino waited until the nurse left, then sat down on the bed next to Megan. "Something tells me if we don't make a run for it, we'll be spending the next few hours explaining your 'miraculous recovery.'"

Megan lifted the sheet and looked down the length of her body. "I don't understand it myself," she said, looking up over the edge of the sheet. "Did you do this?"

"My powers are much more mundane now."

The sheet fell as Megan trailed a fingertip along the top of Gino's thigh. "Oh, I don't know about that."

He smiled. "You're going to get me in trouble with Nurse Hatchett again."

Megan laughed, the sound rivaling the most wondrous musical piece ever composed. "I think a great, big, wet one was exactly what she needed."

"Sorry," Gino declined. "My days of battling beasts are over. My guess is Ishtar took away your injuries."

As if in answer, sunlight slanted beneath the half-mast blinds and fell on the two lovers in a warm golden glow.

"Let's go home." Gino stood and walked toward the narrow metal closet.

Megan, sitting up in the bed, said, "I still can't

believe it about Elliot. I suppose he had it all figured out in his head so it made sense, but did he really think he could get away with it?''

''He almost did,'' Gino pointed out.

''Still, I know he didn't mean to hurt anyone. I'd really like to help him.''

''We will, honey. When we get home, I'll make some calls—one to a businessman I know who gets a kick out of turning around falling enterprises, another to a hotshot lawyer who may be able to get Elliot off with just financial restitution and community service.''

Megan smiled. ''I'm impressed.''

''It pays to have ex-masters in high places.'' Gino pulled back the metal door, exposing the closet's empty insides. ''But before we can do anything, we've got to get you some clothes.''

Wrapping the sheet around her, Megan got up and went to the closet. ''Kinda makes you miss the good ol' days when you could just blink me into something.'' She twisted the sheet tighter around her. ''Maybe nobody will even notice.''

''Nobody but the crowd of newspeople hanging around the hospital. If they see you walking out of here like this, we're talking more exposure than a hospital gown. Listen, wait here. I'll see if I can find us some scrubs or something. I'll be right back.''

When the door opened a minute later, Megan turned toward it with relief. ''Gi...'' The name died on her lips.

''Miss Kelly, I understand you're feeling better?''

the doctor said louder than necessary as if to fill the room with his competent bearing. The nurse was behind him.

Megan sank down onto the bed.

"Still a little weak?" the doctor observed, setting down her chart. "Let's have a look, shall we?"

He listened to her heart, her lungs, pressed on her abdomen, tested her reflexes, even his professionally hearty expression unable to hide his astonishment.

"It's impossible, isn't it?" the nurse asked.

Megan spoke for the first time. "Nothing's impossible."

The doctor studied her from over the edge of the chart. "I'm going to order a few tests, but if those show nothing—"

"Tests?" Megan protested. "I feel fine. I want to go home."

"If the tests show nothing, you will," the doctor promised, turning on his heel and leaving before further argument.

Less than two minutes later, a gurney was wheeled into Megan's room. "I'm not going," she declared.

"Megan?" Gino pulled down the surgeon's mask covering the lower half of his face.

"Thank goodness, it's you." She rushed to him, hugging him with relief. "I thought you were here to take me to the tests my doctor ordered. I think he wants to make me a medical guinea pig for miracle cures."

"We better move fast. I already heard some orderlies talking about the miracle patient. If the newspeople get wind of this, we'll never get out of here. Here, slip this on.'' He handed her a hospital gown and robe. ''Kitty is going to help us.''

''Kitty?''

''Remember, I told you she was with me in the waiting room. She's agreed to create a diversion at the main entrance, giving us enough time to sneak out one of the other exits, but, first, she wants to see you. Hop on.'' He indicated the gurney. ''She's waiting in the visitors' bathroom right down the hall.''

She lay down on the stretcher, and he covered her with a sheet and wheeled her down the hall without incident.

''Okay,'' he bent down and whispered when they were outside the visitors' bathroom. ''I'll wait out here.''

Megan knocked lightly on the bathroom door, then went in. Kitty clasped her in a warm hug.

''Megan!'' She held her out at arm's length, inspecting her. ''You're really okay, just like Gino said.''

''Yes, I'm more than fine. How are you?'' Megan's gaze dropped to Kitty's stomach.

Kitty placed a hand on her belly. ''Still somewhere between shock and rapture.''

Megan laughed softly. ''Believe me, I know the feeling.''

There were two sharp raps on the door, then Gino's urgent voice. ''An orderly asking 'Where's the Kelly patient?' just left the nurses' station. It's time we headed home.''

"Are you going to help us, Kitty?" Megan asked.

"You bet I will."

The two friends hugged each other hard.

"Megan," Kitty said as Megan reached for the door. "He is a genie, isn't he?"

Megan smiled. "He's something far more magical than that...he's the man I love." She opened the door, revealing Gino.

Megan squeezed Kitty's hand.

"Good luck!" Kitty wished.

"Thanks," Megan mouthed as Gino ushered her toward the exit at the end of the hall.

Once in the safety of the empty stairwell, Gino stopped, looked up the stairs, then down, finally meeting Megan's expectant gaze.

"You were expecting a magic carpet maybe?" he asked her.

She laughed like a happy child, then wrapped her arms around his middle and closed her eyes, knowing only the warmth of his flesh. "I suppose this isn't the right time to get romantic?"

He tucked a finger under her chin, tipping her head back, his eyes loving as his head descended toward her. "There could never be a wrong time, Megan."

As their lips were about to meet, they heard the footsteps coming down the stairs.

He kissed her once, twice, then with their arms still wrapped around each other, they hurried down the stairs. Three flights down, they heard voices coming up the stairs. They ducked out into the hall. Signs and arrows painted on the wall directed the way to the hospital's services: Outpatient, Ob/Gyn, Internal Medicine, Pediatrics. In bold red letters at the bottom was printed Emergency Room. A bright red arrow pointed right.

"Of course," Gino said, following the direction of the arrow. "We'll just leave the same way we came in."

"I thought you told me you flew here from the Upper Realm?"

"Okay, we'll leave the way you came in." Gino led her across the emergency room waiting area and through the automatic doors to outside the hospital. Parked in the discharge area were several ambulances. Gino started toward the one parked farthest away from the hospital entrance.

He looked around, then crouched down behind its back door, motioning Megan to do the same.

"There's got to be a law against this somewhere," she whispered.

He slowly opened the back door enough for Megan to climb in. He followed, shutting the door securely after him.

"We can fit under there," he suggested, indicating a lengthy crawl space beneath a wheeled cot.

Megan wriggled into the narrow space, turning so her back was against the wall. Gino eased in beside her. Facing each other, their bodies pressed together, their mouths mere millimeters from each other, they smiled.

"Hi," Gino whispered softly.

"Hi," Megan returned just as reverently. It wasn't

until his fingertip touched her cheek, and she saw the look of concern on Gino's features, did she realize she was crying.

"What's wrong?" he asked worriedly.

She shook her head, smiling through her own tears. "That's the last word I ever expected to hear from you."

Understanding smoothed his features. "You were always expecting me to say goodbye?"

She nodded mutely.

"But I never did, did I?"

"No." It was no more than a breath.

His hands cradled her face. "And I never will, Megan." He kissed away her tears.

Yet, they continued to fall, her happiness now so great it had to take on physical form. As if her joy had grown wings and taken flight, the ambulance's siren sounded and lights began to flash.

She snuggled closer to the man who had brought her so much magic. "So," she asked, as the ambulance began to carry them away. "What do you think of being human?"

The flashing lights were now in his eyes, illuminating emotion so strong, so deep, older than the gods above. He answered her question just before their mouths met:

"It's more than I ever wished for."

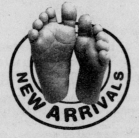

If you enjoyed what you just read,
then we've got an offer you can't resist!

Take 2 bestselling
love stories FREE!
Plus get a FREE surprise gift!

Clip this page and mail it to Harlequin Reader Service®

IN U.S.A.	**IN CANADA**
3010 Walden Ave.	P.O. Box 609
P.O. Box 1867	Fort Erie, Ontario
Buffalo, N.Y. 14240-1867	L2A 5X3

YES! Please send me 2 free Harlequin American Romance® novels and my free surprise gift. Then send me 4 brand-new novels every month, which I will receive months before they're available in stores. In the U.S.A., bill me at the bargain price of $3.34 plus 25¢ delivery per book and applicable sales tax, if any*. In Canada, bill me at the bargain price of $3.71 plus 25¢ delivery per book and applicable taxes**. That's the complete price and a savings of over 10% off the cover prices—what a great deal! I understand that accepting the 2 free books and gift places me under no obligation ever to buy any books. I can always return a shipment and cancel at any time. Even if I never buy another book from Harlequin, the 2 free books and gift are mine to keep forever. So why not take us up on our invitation. You'll be glad you did!

154 HEN CNEX
354 HEN CNEY

Name	(PLEASE PRINT)	
Address	Apt.#	
City	State/Prov.	Zip/Postal Code

* Terms and prices subject to change without notice. Sales tax applicable in N.Y.
** Canadian residents will be charged applicable provincial taxes and GST.
   All orders subject to approval. Offer limited to one per household.
   ® are registered trademarks of Harlequin Enterprises Limited.

AMER99   ©1998 Harlequin Enterprises Limited

#765 THE RIGHT MAN by Anne Stuart
Gowns of White
Five days before Susan Abbott's wedding and she hadn't a thing to
wear. That is until the too-darn-sexy and enigmatic Jake hand delivered an
heirloom wedding gown—and changed her prim and proper, well-planned
life forever.

#766 DADDY'S LITTLE COWGIRL by Charlotte Maclay
Sexy Single Dads
Bad boy turned rancher Reed Drummond had one goal—adopt the tiny
baby girl with whom he'd been entrusted. But to do that, he needed
respectable Ann Forrester to be his wife for a while—or until death do
them part!

#767 BABY FOR HIRE by Liz Ireland
Ross Templeton figured the star baby-model and her nun guardian were
the perfect make-believe daughter and wife he needed. Little did he
know baby Felicity was a terror and that underneath "Sister" Alison's
fake habit beat the heart of a vivacious, sexy woman who could threaten
his bachelor status!

#768 CAN'T RESIST A COWBOY by Jo Leigh
City girl Taylor Reed spared few words for cowboys—arrogant and
pig-headed. She'd come to Zach Baldwin's ranch to prove that cowboys
and marriage didn't mix—and no broad-shouldered, lean-hipped,
sexier-than-he-should-be cowboy was talking her out of it!

Look us up on-line at: http://www.romance.net